### BEAUTY AND THE BEASTS

*She was sitting shyly by the piano, looking at her brother behind his book, when the door burst open most unceremoniously, and three young men stood on the threshold.*

*To be sure, they knocked uproariously upon the opening door, and their greeting was loud and hilarious. Margaret arose, startled. But they stopped as suddenly as they had begun and looked about upon the strange, changed place. This was a room with which they were unacquainted, despite the many times they had ascended the hill to make good cheer for Stephen. And the woman who stood silently by the piano was a lady and was beautiful beyond any question.*

*It was as if they had come expecting summer weather and were suddenly plunged into a magnificent snowbank.*

# BECAUSE OF STEPHEN

Living Books ®
Tyndale House Publishers, Inc.
Wheaton, Illinois

This Tyndale House book
by Grace Livingston Hill
contains the complete text
of the original hardcover edition.
NOT ONE WORD
HAS BEEN OMITTED.

Copyright © 1994 by Tyndale House Publishers
All rights reserved
Cover illustration copyright © 1993 by Corbert Gauthier

*Living Books* is a registered trademark of Tyndale House
Publishers, Inc.

Library of Congress Catalog Card Number 94-60594
ISBN 0-8423-1320-6

01   00   99   98   97   96   95   94
6    5    4    3    2    1

# *A Letter with a Surprise in It*

THE ROOM was full of blue smoke from bacon sizzling on the stove when Philip Earle came in.

Philip was hungry, but there was a weirdly monotonous reminder of preceding meals in the odor of the bacon that took the edge from his appetite.

The lamp was doing its best to help both the smoke and the odor that filled the room; any other function it might have had being held in abeyance by the smoke.

The lamp was on a little shelf on the wall, and under it, half hidden by the smoke, stood another young man bending over the stove.

There was nothing attractive about the room. It was made of rough boards: walls, floor, and ceiling. The furniture was an old extension table, several chairs, a cheap cot covered with a gray army blanket, and a desk which showed hard usage, piled high with papers and a few books. A wooden bench over by the stove held a tin wash-basin and cooking-utensils in harmonious proximity.

Several coats and hats and a horse-blanket hung on nails driven into the walls. A line of boots and shoes stood against the base-board. There was nothing else but a barrel and several boxes.

The table was set for supper: that is, it held a loaf of bread, two cups and knives and spoons, a bag of crackers, a paper of cheese, a pitcher of water, and a can of baked beans newly opened.

Philip added to the confusion already on the table by throwing his bundles down at one end. Then he stood his whip in one corner, and tossed his felt hat across the room to the cot, where it lay as if accustomed to staying where it landed.

"A letter for you, Steve!" he said as he sat down at the table and ran his hands wearily through his thick black hair.

Stephen Halstead emerged from the cloud of smoke by the stove, and examined the postmark on the letter.

"Well, I guess it can wait till we've had supper," he said carelessly. "It's not likely to be important. I'm hungry!" and he landed a large plate of smoking bacon and shrivelled, blackened, fried eggs on the table beside the coffee-pot, and sat down.

They began to eat, silent for the most part, with keen appetites, for both had been in the open air all day. Stephen knew that his partner would presently report about the sale of cattle he had made, and tell of his weary search for several stray animals that had wandered off. But that could wait.

Philip, however, was thinking of something else. Perhaps it was the texture of the envelope he had just laid down, or the whiff of violet scent that had breathed from it as he took it from his pocket, that reminded him of old days; or perhaps it was just that he was hungry and dissatisfied.

"Say, Steve," said he, setting down his empty cup, "do you remember the banquet in '95?"

A cloud came over Stephen's face. He had reasons to remember it of which his friend knew not.

"What of it?" he growled.

"Nothing; only I was thinking I would like to have the squabs and a few other little things

I didn't eat that night. They wouldn't taste bad after a day such as we've had."

He helped himself to another piece of cheese, and took another supply of baked beans.

Stephen laughed harshly. He did not like to be reminded of that banquet night. To create a diversion, he reached out for the letter.

"This is from that precious sister of mine, I suppose," he said, "who isn't my sister at all, and yet persists every once in a while in keeping up the appearance. I don't know what she ever expects to make out of it. I haven't anything to leave her in my will. Besides, I don't answer her letters once in an age."

"You're a most ungrateful dog," said Philip. "You ought to be glad to have some one in the world to write to you. I've often thought of advertising for somebody who'd be a sister to me, at least enough of one to write to me. It would give a little zest to life. I don't see why you have such a prejudice against her. She never did anything. She couldn't help it that her mother was your father's second wife. It wasn't her affair, at all, nor yours either, as I see. When did you see her last?"

"Never saw her but once in my life, and then she was a little, bawling, red thing with long clothes, and everybody waiting on her."

"How old were you?"

"About ten," said Stephen doggedly, not joining in the hilarious laughter that Philip raised at his expense. "I was old enough to resent her being there at all, in my home, where I ought to have been, and her mother managing things and having me sent off to boarding-school to get rid of me. I could remember my own mother, Phil. She hadn't been dead a year when father married again."

"Well, it wasn't her fault anyway, that I can see," said Philip amusedly; "and, after all, she's your sister. She's as much your father's child as you are."

"She's nothing but a half-sister," said Stephen decidedly, "and of no interest in the world to me. What on earth she's taken to writing me long letters for I can't make out. It's only since father died she's done it. I suppose her mother thought it would be well to appease me, lest I make trouble about the will; but I knew well enough there wouldn't be much of anything father had for me. His precious second wife did me out completely from the first minute she set eyes on me. And she's dead now, too. If it hadn't been for what my mother left, I wouldn't have had a cent."

"Who's the girl living with?" asked Philip.

"O, with an aunt,—her mother's sister,—an old maid up in New England."

Then Stephen tore open the letter, and shoved his chair back nearer to the lamp. There was silence in the room while Stephen read his letter; and Philip, emptying the coffee-pot, mused over the life of an orphan girl in the home of a New England maiden aunt.

Suddenly Stephen's chair jerked about with a sharp thud on the bare floor, and Stephen stood up and uttered some strong language.

He had a lot of light hair, originally a golden brown, but burnt by exposure to sun and rain to a tawny shade. He was a slender fellow, well knit, with a complexion tanned to nature's own pleasant brown, out of which looked deep, unhappy eyes of blue. He would have been handsome but for a restless weakness about the almost girlish mouth.

He was angry now, and perplexed. His yellow brows were knit together in a frown, his head up, and his eyes darker than usual. Philip watched him in languid amusement, and waited for an explanation.

"Well, is she too sisterly this time?" he asked.

"Altogether!" said Stephen. "She's coming to see us."

The amusement passed rapidly from Philip's

face. He sprang to his feet, while the color rolled up under his dark skin.

"Coming to see *us?*" he ejaculated, looking round and suddenly seeing all the short-comings of the room.

"Coming to see *us?*" he repeated as if not quite sure of the sound of his own words. *"Here?"*

"Here!" asseverated Stephen tragically with outspread hands, and the two looked about in sudden knowledge of the desolation of the place they had called "home" for three years.

"When?" Philip managed to murmur weakly, looking about in his mind for a way of escape for himself without deserting his partner.

Stephen stooped to pick up the letter he had thrown on the floor in his excitement.

"I don't know," he said dejectedly. "Here, read the thing, and see if you can find out." He handed the letter to Philip, who received it with alacrity, and settled into the chair under the light, suddenly realizing that he was tired.

"She'll have to be stopped," said Stephen meditatively, sitting down on the cot to study it out, "or sent back if it's too late for stopping. She can't come *here,* of course."

"Of course!" agreed Philip decidedly. Then he read:

*"My dear Brother Stephen:—"*

Philip suddenly felt strong jealousy of his friend. It would be nice to get a letter like that.

"It is a long time since I have been able to write to you, but you have never been out of my thoughts for long at a time. Aunt Priscilla was taken ill the day after I wrote you the last time. She was confined to her room all winter, and some of the time a little flighty. She took queer notions. One of them was that I was going to run away and marry a Spaniard. She could not bear me out of her sight. This tied me down very much, even though we had a nurse who relieved me of the entire care of her. I could not even write when I was in her sight, because she imagined I was getting up some secret plot to send her away to an old ladies' home of which she had a great horror.

"I don't like to think of those long, dreary months; but they are all over now, and I will not weary you with talking of them. Aunt Priscilla died a month ago, and now I am all alone in the world save for you. Stephen, I wonder if you have any idea how dear you have grown to me. Sometimes it has seemed as if I just could not wait any longer to see you. It has kept me up wonderfully to know that I have a lovely, big, grown-up brother to turn to."

Philip's eyes grew moist, and he stopped to clear his throat as he turned the page and glanced surreptitiously toward the unloving brother, who sat in a brown and angry study, his elbows on his knees, his chin in his hands.

"So now, Stephen, I am going to do just what I have wanted to do ever since mother died and I left college and came home to Aunt Priscilla. I am coming to you! There is nothing to hinder. I have sold the old house. There was a good opportunity, and I cannot bear the place. It has been desolate, desolate here." Philip wondered what she would think of her brother's home. "I cannot bear the thought of staying here alone, and I know I could not coax you away from your beloved West. So I am all packed up now, except the things that have been sold, and I am starting at once. Perhaps you may not like it, may not want me; and in that case of course I can come back. But anyway I shall see you first. I could not stand it without seeing you. I keep thinking of what father said to me just before he died. I never told you. I have always thought I would rather wait till I could say it to you, but now I will send it on to you as my plea for a welcome. It was the last afternoon we had together. Mother was lying down, and I was alone with him. He had been asleep, and he suddenly opened his eyes and called me to him. 'Don't forget you have a brother, when I am gone,' he said, and then after a minute he looked up and said: 'Tell him I'm afraid I wasn't wise in my treatment of him always. Tell him I loved him, and I love you, and I want you two to love each other.'

"I began to love you then, Stephen, and the longing to know you and see you has grown with the years, five years, since father died. I never told mother about it. She was not well enough to talk much, you know; and she did not live long after that. Of course I never told Aunt Priscilla. She was not the kind of woman to whom one told things. But I have never had opportunity to claim that love, or to seek it except in just writing you letters occasionally; and sometimes I've been afraid you didn't care to get them. But now I'm coming to see for myself; and, if I'm not welcome, why, I can go back again. I shall not be a burden to you, brother; for I have enough, you know, to take care of myself. And, if you don't want me, all you have to do is to tell me so, and I can go away again. But I hope you'll be able to love me a little for father's sake."

"Have you read the whole of this, Steve?" asked Philip, suddenly looking up as he reached the end of one sheet of paper and was starting on another.

"No," said Stephen gruffly; "I read enough."

"Read the rest," commanded Philip, handing over the first sheet while he went on with the second.

"Now I have burned my bridges behind me, Stephen; and I have not let you know until just the last thing. This letter will reach you only a few days before I do; so it will not be of any use to telegraph me not to come if you don't want me, for I shall be well on my way, and it will be too late. Please forgive me; I did this purposely because I felt I must at least see you before I gave up my plan, or I should never be able to give it up. And I am hoping that you will be glad to see me, and that perhaps I can be of some use to you, and put a little comfort into your life. You have never told me whether you are boarding or housekeeping or what. It is strange not to know more about one's brother than I do about mine, but I shall soon know now. I am bringing all the little things I care about with me; so, if you let me stay, I shall have nothing to send for; and, if I have to go back, they can go back, too, of course.

"I shall reach your queer-sounding station at eight o'clock Friday evening, and I hope you will be able to meet me at the train, for of course I shall be very lonely in a strange place. Forgive me for surprising you this way. I know Aunt Priscilla would think I was doing a dreadful thing; but I can't feel that way about it myself, and anyway I have myself to look out for now. So good-by until Friday evening of next week, and please make up your mind to be a little glad to see your sister,"

*"Margaret Halstead."*

Philip handed over the last sheet to Stephen, and sat up, looking blankly at the wall for a minute. He could not deny to himself that he was wholly won over to the enemy's cause. There was something so fresh and appealing about that letter written from a lonely girlish heart, and something so altogether brave and daring in her actually starting out to hunt up a renegade brother who had shown no wish to be brotherly, that he could but admire her. But what could they do with her there? Of course she must go back. A pity, too, when she seemed to have her heart so set. But, if she stayed, she would be disappointed. Philip looked at Stephen sadly. It was a good thing she must go back, and would not need to know how little

worthy of her love and admiration this unknown brother of hers was. He was a good-
hearted fellow, too. A pity for the girl she had
not some one to care for her.

Suddenly a new thought came to him as he
looked idly down at the envelope of the letter
Stephen had carelessly flung aside. The date on
it was a week old.

He picked it up excitedly.

"Steve, what day was that letter written?"

"The twenty-eighth," said Stephen, looking
up to see what caused the unusual note in
Philip's tone.

"Man alive!" exclaimed Philip, "that letter's
lain in the office for more than a week now, or
else it's been off up to Humstead's ranch, lying
around till some one had time to bring it back
to the office. Such a postmaster as they have
out here anyway! Get up, Steve, and do something! *This* is Friday night! Don't you realize
that your sister's almost here? If it wasn't that
the Northern Central is always an hour or
more behind time, she would be standing
alone down there on the platform, in the dark,
this minute, with all that howling mob of
loungers that congregate near by. What are you
going to do?"

"I don't know," said Stephen in a dazed way.

Philip towered over him fiercely.

"Well, you *better* know. Get up. It's five miles away, and the express is due now if it's on time."

2

## *A Strange Night Ride*

MARGARET Halstead stood alone on the narrow board platform that seemed to float like a tiny raft in a sea of plains and darkness.

The train on which she had come her long and interesting journey had discharged her trunks, and taken up some freight, and wound its snakelike way out into the darkness, until now even the last glimmer of its red lights had faded from the mist that lay around.

The night winds swept about her, touching hair and cheek and gown, and peering solicitously into her face as if to inquire who this strange, sweet thing might be that had dropped, alien, among them, and then, deciding in her favor, softly kissed her on the cheek and ran away to tell the river of her coming.

A few lights dotted here and there the murk

and gloom about her, and loud, uncultured voices sounded from the little shanty that served, she supposed, as a station. She dreaded to move a step toward it, for a strange new terror had seized upon her in the darkness since the friendly train had disappeared from view.

She remembered that the porter had been solicitous about leaving until her brother arrived to claim her, and had paused beside her until the last car swept slowly up and began to travel by; then, eying dubiously first the silver piece she had put in his hand, and then the fast-gliding train, he had finally touched his cap and swung himself onto the last car, calling back to her that he hoped she would be all right. She had not realized till then what it was going to be to be left alone at night in this strange place, with no assurance whatever, save her own undaunted faith, that her brother had even received her letter, much less, would meet her.

Apprehension and alarm suddenly rose and began to clamor for attention, while she suddenly realized how rash she had been to follow a fancy half across a continent, only to bring up in this wild way.

What should she do? She supposed she ought to go over to that dreadful group of rough men and ask some questions. What if, after all, she had been put off at the wrong station? She half turned to walk in that direction; but just then a wild shriek followed by a pistol-shot rang out in the air, and she stopped, frightened, a whispered prayer on her lips for help. Had she come all this way on what her heart had told her was a mission, to be forsaken now?

The clamor was heard by Philip as he rode through the night.

Stephen heard it also, and hastened his horse's footsteps.

Then from out the gloom and horror there came to the young girl's ears the soft regular thud, thud, thud, of horses' hoofs, and almost at once there loomed before her out of the mist two dark shapes which flung themselves apart, and appeared to be two men and two horses.

She started back once more, her heart beating wildly, and wondered which way to flee; but almost at once she heard a strong, pleasant voice say:

"Don't be afraid. We are coming!" and what seemed a giant landed before her. With a little gasp in her voice that sounded like a half-sob she said,

"O Stephen, you have come!" and put her

hands in those of Philip Earle, hiding her face against his shoulder with a shudder.

Philip felt a sudden gladness in his strength, and it was revealed to him in a flash that there were sweeter things in life than those he had counted upon.

Instinctively his arm supported her for just an instant, and a great wave of jealousy toward her brother went over him. His impulse was to stoop and give her the welcoming kiss that she was evidently expecting; but he held himself with a firm grasp, though the blood went in hot waves over his face in the darkness.

To have the unexpected and most unwelcome guest of his partner thus suddenly precipitated upon him, and to find that she was not altogether undesirable, after all, was a circumstance most embarrassing, as well as extremely delicate to handle. He blessed the darkness for its hiding. It was but an instant and Stephen was beside them, and he managed in some way—he never could describe it to himself afterward—to get the young woman faced about toward the real brother and her attention turned in that direction, and then stood watching while Stephen, the impressible, welcomed the new sister with open arms.

It was like Stephen, though he had grumbled all the way to the railroad about what a nuisance it was going to be to have her come, that he should succumb at once to a sweet voice and a confiding way.

Philip's lips were dry, and his throat throbbed hot and chokingly. He felt the pressure of little, soft, gloved hands in his hard ones. He turned away angry with himself that he should be so easily affected and by some one whom he had never met except in the pitch dark. Yet even as he said this to himself he knew the face would fit the voice and the hands when he should see them.

So, after all, though Philip, because he rode the fleeter horse, had been the first to greet her, and though his was the cool head, and he had expected to have to explain why they had been so late to meet her, it was Stephen's eager voice that made the explanations.

"You see I never got your letter until an hour ago. It was miscarried or something, and then we don't get to the office often when we're busy. So, when I took it in that you were really coming and looked at the time, your train was already overdue; and, if it had not been for their habit of being always two hours behind time, you might have stood here alone all this time."

Stephen said it gayly. He was beginning to think it a nice thing to have a sister. He had forgotten utterly how Philip had to insist on his coming at once to meet her, and that he had been most reluctant and ungracious.

It occurred to him at this juncture to introduce his partner.

Philip came to himself as he heard his name mentioned, and was glad again for the darkness. Margaret Halstead blushed, and wondered whether this giant knew how extremely near she had come to greeting him with a kiss, and hoped that he had not noticed how her head had rested against his shoulder for an instant when she was frightened. What would he think of her?

Her voice trembled just a little as she acknowledged the introduction; but her words were few and frigid, and made Philip feel as if she had suddenly held him off at arm's length and bade him come no nearer. She said:

"I did not know you had a partner, Stephen. You never said anything about it in your letters. I am afraid I have been wrong in coming without waiting to hear from you before I started."

But Philip had noticed the tremble in her voice, and he hastened to make her most welcome as far as he was concerned.

Nevertheless, a stiffness hung about the trio which made it hard for them to be natural; and, had it not been for another pistol-shot from the shanty down the road and another clamor of voices, they might have stood still some time longer.

Margaret started in spite of herself, and asked nervously:

"Oh! what can be the matter? What a dreadful place this must be!" And Philip found in himself a new instinct of protection.

"We must get your sister out of this, Steve," he said. "We must take her home."

And somehow the word "home" sounded a haven as he pronounced it. The thoughts of the two young men galloping furiously on their way to the station had been but of how they should reach there as soon as the train. They had made no plans. It was impossible for them to realize the importance of the charge that was about to be put upon them.

But now the manners of the world from which they had come some years before, and from which this young woman had but just come, suddenly dropped down upon them as a forgotten garment, and they knew at once the wretchedness of their limitations.

"It isn't much of a place to call home," said

the brother, apologetically, "but I guess it's better than this. If we had only known before, we'd have had something fine fixed up someway."

He made the statement airily, and perhaps he thought it was true. Philip found himself wondering what it would have been. There was not a house where she might have been lodged comfortably within fifty miles.

"How do you think we'd better arrange the journey?" said Stephen, suddenly brought face to face with a problem.

"You see," said he in explanation to his sister, "we had no time to hitch up, if we had thought of it, though I'm blamed if it occurred to me but that we could carry you in our pockets. Say, Phil, guess I'll go over and see if I can get Foxy's buckboard."

"Foxy's gone over to Butte in his buckboard with his mother. I saw him go this afternoon," answered Philip.

Stephen whistled.

"I'll ask Dunn for his wagon," said Stephen starting off.

"Hold on!" said Philip shortly. "I'll go myself. You stay here."

"Couldn't we go down to the station and see after my trunk, Mr. Earle?" said Margaret timidly. And to his ears the name never had so sweet a sound.

"Give me your checks, and stay here, please," he said in quite a different tone from that in which he had addressed Stephen; and, turning, he left them standing in the dark, while the mist closed in behind him and shut him from their sight as if he had left the world.

Alone with her brother, Margaret suddenly put out her hands appealingly to him.

"You are a little bit glad I've come, aren't you, Stephen?" she said.

"I'm no end of glad," he answered, rousing out of his sulkiness that Philip would not let him go. He knew that Philip had good reason for making him stay. "But we're a rough lot out here. I don't know how you'll stand it."

His voice had lost a shade of the gayety, and she thought it was touched with anxiety. She hastened to assure him.

"O, I shall not mind a bit. And I shall try to make things a little pleasanter for you. You think I can, don't you?" This in an anxious voice.

"I'm sure you can," said Stephen heartily. There was something in her voice that appealed to his better self, and reminded him strangely of his childhood. It could not be his father; for his father had always been silent and grave, and this voice was sweet and enthusiastic, and flowed out as if it loved to speak. And yet it must be the likeness to the father's voice he noticed.

"I am so anxious to get you in the light and see how you look," she said ardently, and then added softly, "My dear brother."

Stephen slid his arm about her awkwardly, and kissed her on the forehead. He felt embarrassed in doing this; yet it was by no means the first time he had kissed a girl. Perhaps it was the memory of those other kisses hovering near that shamed him now. He half felt this, and it made him awkward. He was glad to hear Philip's step coming toward them.

"Dunn's wagon has broken down, and both the front wheels are off for repairs. There isn't a thing we can get in town to-night," said Philip anxiously. "Miss Halstead, can you ride? Horseback, I mean."

"Why, I can try," said Margaret a little tremulously. This was a rather startling proposition to even her dauntless courage. Involuntarily she glanced down at her city-made gown in the darkness. She felt hampered by it.

"It's too bad, Miss Halstead," he said apologetically, while Stephen in the dark wondered at his new tone and manner. "But there's no other way, and I think you'll enjoy getting out of this, anyway. There's going to be a big row over there," he added in a low tone to Stephen. "Jim Peters is on his high horse. Hurry!"

Then in a cheery tone he said:

"It won't be so bad. You can rest your foot in the stirrup, and Steve and I'll take turns walking beside the horse. She'd better ride your horse, Steve. He's the gentler of the two."

Margaret Halstead felt herself suddenly lifted in the dark by strong arms and seated on a horse. She clung to the saddle, and left her foot obediently in the stirrup where it was placed by a firm hand; but she was not certain whether her brother or his friend had put her there. It was bewildering, all in the dark that way, and neither of them spoke till both were standing by her side. She was glad the horse stood quite still. She expected him to start nervously. She felt timid about Western horses. They had a reputation for wildness. But it was Stephen who after a moment of low talk came and stood by her side and placed his arm about her as they started.

"My suit-case and my bag," she murmured.

"Phil has them all safe," said her brother.

"And the trunks?"

"They are locked safe in the station, Miss Halstead, and we will get them early in the morning," said a voice out of the mist before her.

Then there was silence as she looked anxiously into the darkness, and could not see a spot of road for the horse to place his foot.

The road was rough and her seat unsteady. A man's saddle is not the surest thing to ride sideways upon. She put her hand timidly on her brother's shoulder, and the touch seemed to give her courage. It gave Stephen a strange new sense of his power of protection.

They went slowly, for the night was dark and the mist lay thick about them. The road was so rough that horse and leader could keep together only by moving slowly. The sounds of disturbance behind them grew fainter as they went on, but now and then a shriek or a fragment of an oath would reach them as if it had been flung out wildly in the night and lost its way.

Margaret shuddered when this happened, and said in a half-frightened tone:

"What awful people they must be, Stephen! Isn't it unpleasant to live in their neighborhood?"

And Stephen somewhat uneasily answered: "O, they never bother us. They've got a little too much to-night, that's all; and, when they get like that, they can't stand a difference of opinion."

"How dreadful!" said Margaret in low, awestruck tones. Then after a minute she added:

"O Stephen, I'm so glad my brother is not like that. Of course it wouldn't be likely, but they must be somebody's brothers, and how their sisters must feel—and their mothers!"

Stephen felt his face grow hot. He said nothing for a long time. He could not think of anything to say. There was a strange feeling about his throat, and he tried to clear it. The mist kept getting in his eyes. He was glad when his sister began to tell of her aunt's illness and the long, weary months when she had been chained to the sick-room at the beck and call of a whimsical, wandering mind.

She did not say much about herself, but he felt touched by her sweet self-sacrifice and her loneliness. It reminded him of his own lonely boyhood, and his heart went out in sympathy. He decided that it was a nice thing, after all, to have a sister. It was like Stephen to forget all about the end of their journey and the poor accommodations he had to offer her, utterly unfit for a woman, much less fit for one who had been brought up in luxury. He grew gay as they went on, and talked more freely with her. When Philip suddenly appeared out of the silent darkness ahead of them, and said it was time to change guides, he was almost loath to leave his sister.

Margaret, too, would rather not have had the change; but she could scarcely ask her brother to walk the whole of the five miles. There was something about him that reminded her, even in the dark, of their father, and so he did not seem strange; but this other tall man, who had taken control of the entire expedition, frightened her a little. She wished she could get a glimpse of his face and know what kind of a man he was. It was hard to know what to say to him, and still more embarrassing to keep entirely still.

But the road was growing rougher. The new guide had to give a good deal of attention to the horse, and she to keeping her unsteady seat. The road was steadily rising before them now. She could feel that by the inclination of the saddle. It seemed to be stony also.

Once she slipped, and would have fallen from the saddle if Philip had not caught her. After that he placed his arm about her and steadied her. She could not object, for there was nothing intimate or personal in the touch.

She concluded that Philip was a gentleman, whatever else he might not be.

She gripped the saddle in front of her a little tighter, and looked into the darkness, wondering whether this journey would ever end. She essayed one or two sentences of conversation, but the young man beside her was distraught, and seemed to be more interested in looking ahead and guiding the horse.

The road was even steeper now. Margaret wondered whether they were going up the Rocky Mountains. It seemed as if they had come far enough to have almost reached them, according to her vague notion of the geography of that land.

"Wouldn't it be better if I were to get off and walk?" she asked timidly, after the horse had almost stumbled to his knees.

"No," answered Philip shortly; "we'll soon be over this. Put your arm around my neck and hold on now. Don't be afraid! Steady, there, steady, Jack!"

The horse scrambled, and seemed to Margaret to be walking on his hind legs up into the air. She gave a little scream, and threw her arm convulsively about her companion's neck. But she was held firmly, and seemed to riding upon Philip's shoulder with the horse struggling under her for a moment. Then like a miracle they reached upper ground, and she was sitting firmly on the horse's back, Philip walking composedly beside her, his arm no more about her.

It was lighter too, here; and all the mist seemed to have dropped away and to be melting at their feet.

"It's all over now," said Philip, and there was a joyous ring in his voice quite different from the silent, abstracted man who had walked beside her for so long. "I hope you weren't much frightened. I've been afraid how Jack would act there. That is an ugly place. It must be fixed before you come this way again. You see the bridge was broken down the way we usually go, and we had to come around another way. You were perfectly safe, you know; only it was bad to frighten you when you have just come, and you are tired, too. But we are almost there now. And look! Look ahead!"

Margaret looked, and saw before her a blaze of light flare up till it made a great half-circle on the edge of the horizon. Not until it rose still higher—like a human thing, she thought—did the girl recognize the moon.

"O, it is the moon!" she said awestruck. "Is it always so great out here?"

Philip watched her as she looked. He felt that for the first time in his life he had companionship in this great sight of which he never tired.

"It is always different," he said musingly, "and yet always the same," and he felt as he was saying it that she would understand. He had never talked to Stephen about the moon. Stephen did not care for such things except as they were for his personal convenience or pleasure. Moonlight might be interesting if one had a long ride to take, in Stephen's economics, but not for purposes of sentiment.

"I see," said Margaret. "Yes, I recognize my old friend now. It seems as if it wore a smile of welcome."

"Do you mean the man in the moon, or the lady? Which do you claim?"

"O, both!" laughed Margaret, turning toward him for the first time since there had been any light. And now she could see his fine profile outlined against the moon, the firm chin, the well-moulded forehead and nose, and the curve of the expressive lips.

"Now, look down there, back where we have come!" said Philip, as she looked.

The mist was glorified like an expectant

one waiting to be redeemed from the state where it was put till its work was done.

"O!" breathed the girl in wonder. "You can fairly see the darkness flee away!"

"So you can," said Philip, looking off. "I never noticed that before."

And they started forward round the turn in the road where Stephen was waiting impatiently for them to come up with him, and almost at once they saw before them the outlines of the rude building the two young men called home, lying bathed in the new-risen moonlight.

# Margaret Makes Herself at Home

THE MOONLIGHT was doing its best to gild the place with something like beauty to welcome the stranger, but it was effective only out-of-doors, and the two young men were painfully conscious of the state in which they had left the inside of their house, as they helped their guest from the horse and prepared to take her in. All the impossibility of the situation suddenly came upon them both, and made them silent and embarrassed.

Stephen took on his sulky look, which ill became him, while he stumbled over the moonbeams that followed him when he opened the door, and lighted the wicked little oil lamp. He had no mind to welcome his sister there. What did he want of a sister anyway? His foot caused the crisp rattle of paper as he threw the match down, and he knew it was her letter lying on the floor. The same mood that had seized him when he read it was upon him again; and he turned, scowling, determined to show her that she had made a serious mistake in rushing out here unbidden.

Margaret Halstead turned from the brilliant moonlight to the blinking lamplight bravely, and faced the scene of her self-chosen mission.

There may have been something in the half-defiant attitude of her brother that turned her from her purpose of having a good long look at him and making sure of her welcome. She may have seen that she had yet to win her way into the citadel of his heart, and wisdom or intuition taught her to break the embarrassment of this first moment in the light by a commonplace remark.

Her eyes roved anxiously about the dreary room in search of something to bring cheer. They fell upon the old desk in the corner.

"O Stephen! There is the desk from your old room!" she cried eagerly, going over to it and touching it tenderly. "I used to go up into your room and sit by it to study my lessons. And sometimes I would put your picture on the top,—the one you sent father when you were in the military school,—and sit, and admire you, and think how nice it was to have a straight, strong brother dressed in a military suit."

Stephen turned toward her with a look of mingled astonishment and admiration. His ugly mood was already exorcised. The soft rustle of hidden silk, made by her garments as she moved, created a new world in the rough place. She stood by the old desk, loosening the hat-pin and taking off her hat; he could see the grace of every movement. And this beautiful girl had cared for him enough to look at his picture once in a while when he was just a boy! He half wished he had known it then; it might have made some things in his life different. His voice was husky as he said, "You don't mean you ever thought of me then, and called me your brother!"

"Yes, surely," she said, looking at him with a bright smile as she ran her fingers through the soft hair over her forehead, and settled it as if by magic into a fitting frame for her sweet face. "O, you don't know how I idealized you! I used to put myself asleep at night with stories about you, of how brave and good and true you were, and how you did all sorts of great things for me—I'll tell you them all some day. But now, do you know you haven't welcomed me home yet? You're sure you're going to be glad I came?"

She looked up anxiously, a sweet pleading in her lovely eyes as she came over to him, and held up her face. Stephen bent over her awkwardly, and kissed her forehead, and then turned away in embarrassment, knocking down the tin basin from the bench as he moved; but Margaret felt she had her welcome, and set herself to win this brother.

Philip would fain have escaped to the barn from the confusion of the first few minutes, but had been drawn back to the door for very shame at deserting his partner in time of embarrassment, and had heard the little dialogue.

He turned silently away from the door, and slipped back to the horses thoughtfully. He had never seen that look on Stephen's face before, nor heard his voice so huskily tender. Perhaps, after all, there was something in a sister.

Margaret Halstead folded her wisp of a veil as carefully and precisely as if she had just come home from a concert in the East, instead of being dropped down in this land that knew her not; but all the while she was taking mental note of the place, its desolation, its need of her, its paucity of material with which to work, and wondering how these two men had lived and been comfortable.

"And now you are hungry," she said in a matter-of-fact tone, just as if her brother were the guest and she the hostess, "and what can we get for supper?"

Stephen had returned from a chase after the tin wash-basin, which had chosen, after the manner of inanimate articles, to take a rattling excursion under the stove. He was looking helplessly about the room. He did not know what he ought to do next.

"There isn't much but bacon and beans, the same old stuff. We have it morning, noon, and night."

Margaret came over to the table and began to gather the dishes together. It was a strange assortment, and she felt like laughing as she extracted the hammer from under the paper of cheese and looked about for a place to lay it; but she kept her face as sober as if that were the proper place for hammers and cheese, and said thoughtfully:

"Haven't you any eggs? I think you mentioned poultry in one of your letters."

"O yes, there are eggs. There are always eggs

and bacon. They would be good if they weren't always the same."

"How would you like an omelet? Do you ever make them?"

"Yes, we've tried, but they lie around in little weary heaps, and won't 'om' for us," said Stephen, laughing at last. "I'll go out and get some eggs if you think you could make one."

"Yes, indeed!" said Margaret with alacrity. "Just show me how this stove works first, and fill the tea-kettle. I always use boiling water for my omelets; it makes them fluffier than milk. Where is your egg-beater kept?"

"Egg-beater!" said Stephen with a shrug of his shoulders. "Don't ask me. I wouldn't know one if I met him on the street. Can't you make an omelet without an egg-beater?" he added anxiously.

"O yes," said Margaret, laughing; "a fork is slower, but it will do. Bring me the eggs now. I will have them ready by the time the kettle boils and the frying-pan is hot."

Margaret worked rapidly while he was gone, and managed to clear the table and wash three plates and cups before he returned. Then she went to her bag that Philip had put just inside the door, and after a little search brought forth four large clean handkerchiefs, a supply of which she usually took with her on a journey. These she spread, one under each plate and one in the centre. At least, it would not seem quite so uncivilized as did that bare table.

An examination into her lunch-box showed a glass of jelly still untouched and half a dozen sugary doughnuts, the farewell contribution of an old neighbor of her aunt's. These she arranged on the table with a plate of bread cut in thin slices, and was just searching for possible coffee when she heard the voices of the two young men.

Stephen went whistling out to the barn for the eggs. "Christopher Columbus, Phil! She knows how to make omelet! Hustle there, and help me get a lot of eggs. We'll have something worth eating again if it takes every egg on the place."

Philip had been wondering whether he might not be excused from going back to the house that night at all. But at the appetizing sound he went to work with a will.

They stopped in astonishment at the door, and gazed at the table as if it had been enchanted, and then gazed anew at the cook. They had left her there a fashionably attired young woman of a world that was theirs now no longer. They found her now a busy woman, with frock daintily tucked up and a white towel pinned about her waist apron-fashion, her sleeves rolled up, revealing white, rounded arms, and her cheeks pink with interest over her work.

"That lamp smokes horribly," she remarked, looking up at it vindictively; and there was something so true and human about her voice and words that both young men laughed.

The stiffness was broken, and did not return; but the relations were established and the guest was commander-in-chief. She told her hosts what to do, and they did it. She took the eggs and deftly broke them, the whites into one dish, the yolks into another; and, giving Stephen one dish with a fork to beat them, she took the other herself, meanwhile commanding Philip to find the coffee and make it.

They enjoyed it as much as three children at play, and their appetites were keen, when a few minutes later, having watched the puffy omelet swell and billow and take on a lovely brown coat, they drew up to the table to supper.

Margaret told little incidents of her journey, and described the people who had been her fellow travellers, showing a rare talent for mimicry, which entertained her audience exceedingly.

It was late when the meal was finally concluded and the room put into what Margaret thought was a poor apology for order. The problem of the night was now to be faced, and Margaret wondered what was to become of her. She suddenly realized how very weary she was, and that her nerves, long overstrained by new experiences, were ready to give way in tears.

Stephen knew that something must be done about sleeping now; but he had no idea what they were going to do with the new sister, any more than if she had been an orphan baby left upon his door-step. He turned helplessly to Philip. Philip always knew what to do in emergencies, though Stephen did not like to admit that he depended upon him.

Philip had done some thinking while he stood by the horses in the moonlight. There was a little log lean-to opening off this large one-roomed cottage of theirs. It was divided by a board partition into two fair-sized rooms. One of these had been Philip's room and the other Stephen's. There was little furniture in them besides a bunk with heavy blankets. Blankets were the only bedclothing the house possessed, and with them beds were easily made. Philip turned toward the door of his room now, and in the dark went about the walls, hastily gathering an armful of clothing from the nails driven into the logs, which he threw out the window. Then he struck a match, and picked up a few things thrown here and there in confusion, and decided that was the best he could do toward clearing up.

He explained to Stephen in a low tone that he was to give his sister that room, and he himself would sleep in the hay. Then, saying good-night, he went out.

Margaret almost laughed aloud when she looked about her primitive bedroom a few minutes later, and by the light of the blinking lamp took an inventory of her surroundings. Then her eye caught a photograph pinned to the wall, and she went over to study it. It was Philip's one possession that he prized, and he had forgotten it in his haste. It was a sweet-faced woman with white hair and eyes like Philip's that followed one about the room sadly.

She had been shocked, even prepared as she was for the primitive, to find her brother living among surroundings so rough. Nevertheless, her determination was firm. She had come to help her brother, and now that she had seen him she would not turn back. There might be some hardships; but in the end, with the help of God, she would win. She felt shy of Philip, and inclined to wish him away. Perhaps he did not have a good influence over Stephen. He seemed to be very dictatorial, and the strange part about it was that Stephen yielded to him. It might be that she would have to help Philip in order to help her brother. That would complicate matters.

She knelt down beside the hard gray cot, and put the work she had come to do at the foot of the cross, asking help and guidance. And she wondered as she prayed whether she had been rash and taken her own way, instead of waiting for heavenly guidance, in coming to this strange land where evidently, to say the least, her presence had not been desired. Then she added, "O Jesus Christ, if this work is of Thee, bless me in it; and, if it was merely a wild impulse of my own, send me back where Thou wouldst have me."

Then with a feeling of contentment she lay down wrapped in the gray blankets, and was almost immediately asleep.

"Is she there?" asked the wind, whispering softly.

"Yes, asleep," said a moonbeam peeping

through a crack between the logs, and then stealing in across the window-ledge.

"And will she stay?" sighed the night wind again.

"Yes, she has come to stay," affirmed the moonbeams, "and she will be a blessing."

Out in the sweet-scented hay lay Philip, but he was not asleep. There was planning to be done for tomorrow. Would the guest choose to stay, or would she fly from them at the morning light? Could she stand it there, so rough and devoid of all that had made her life what it was? Of course not. She had come only on a tour of curiosity. She would probably give it up and go back reasonably in a few days. But in the meantime, unless she came to her senses by morning and knew enough to go back to civilization at once, what was to be done?

In the first place, there must be a woman of some sort found, a servant, if you please. A chaperone she would be called back in the East. Here perhaps such things were not necessary, especially as she was really Stephen's sister; but it would be better to have a woman around. She must not be allowed to do the cooking, and surely they could not cook for her. It had been bad enough for them, men as they were, to eat what they cooked. How good that supper had tasted! The omelet reminded him of his mother, and he drew his hand quickly across his eyes. What would his mother think of his staying out here in the wilds so long? And all because a pretty girl had chosen to flirt with him for a while and then threw him aside. But was it all that? Did he not stay for Stephen's sake? What would become of Stephen without him?

But perhaps, now, Stephen's sister had brought him a release. He might just pretend to have business calling him away and leave them together. Then a vision of the frightened hands that came through the mist to greet him at the station recalled him sharply. No! He could not leave her alone with her brother! It would not do. And at once he knew that his mother, if she were able to know of what went on in this life, would approve of his staying here.

But where was a woman to be found who would be a fit servant for Miss Halstead?

He searched the country in his mind all round and about, and at last came to a conclusion.

The hay settled and crackled about him, and the hens near by clucked anxiously in their sleep; the horses moved against the stall now and then, and away in the distance came the sharp, vigilant bark of a dog. Philip dropped asleep for a little while, and dreamed of a small hand clinging to his neck and a wisp of soft, sweet hair blowing across his face, and awoke to find the hay hanging over and touching his cheek and a warm ray of morning lighting the sky.

The morning was all cool and fresh with sleep yet, when he rose and rode away, hurrying his horse onward through the dewy way. He found himself wondering what Stephen's sister would say to this or that view or bit of woodland that he passed, and then checked his thoughts angrily. She was nothing to him, even if she had understood his thoughts about the moon. Women were all alike, heartless—unless it might be mothers. With these thoughts he flung his horse's bridle over the saddle-horn, and sprang down at the door of a rude dwelling, where after much ado he brought to the door a dark-faced woman with straggling black hair.

What arguments he used or what inducements he offered to bring the curious creature to promise she would come, he never told. But when a half-hour later, with the additional burden of a large, greasy-looking bundle fastened to his saddle, he again started homeward, he smiled faintly to himself, and wondered why he had done it. Perhaps, after all, by this time their guest had made preparations for her departure. And this wild woman with her lowering looks and her muttering speech, would she be any addition to their already curiously assorted family?

A fierce rebellion, often there before, arose in his breast at the Power, whether God or what, that made and kept going a universe so filled with lives awry and hearts of bitterness and sorrow. Not even the breath of the morning, nor the rich notes of wild birds, could quite dispel this from his heart. A sky like that above him, so peerless, and earth like this around him, so matchless, and only lives like his and Stephen's and that dark-faced old hag's to enjoy them. He ran over the whole rough crew of friends who sometimes congregated with them, and saw no good in any.

Still, there was Margaret Halstead. She seemed a fitting one to place amid beauty and joyous surroundings. She would not mar a scene like that this morning with anything her heart or life contained.

Yes, there was Margaret. But it might be only seeming. Perhaps she was like them all.

Doubtless she was. It remained to be seen what Margaret really was. But what were they all made for, anyway?

The old question had troubled Philip for a long, lonely time; and he drew his brows in an unhappy frown as he came to a halt at the only home he now owned.

4

# A Piano in the Wilderness

WHEN Margaret Halstead came to the door a little later to view the morning and look by daylight upon the new land into which she had come a stranger and a pilgrim, she still carried with her the atmosphere of her Eastern home. She had changed the long, dark, close-fitting travelling-gown of the night before to a simple gown of light percale which she had wisely brought in her hand-baggage; and, though the garment was plain and of walking length, and must have occupied little space in the satchel, it hung with a grace and finish unknown in those parts; and there was still about her as she moved that soft atmosphere of refinement.

She opened the door wide, and stood for a moment enframed. The dark, big-boned creature who was huddled on the steps sprang up and gazed at her in wonder. Her eyes had never met a sight like this before. The golden hair, touched with the sunshine into finer threads of spun glass, the blue eyes like rare stones that hold the colors of a summer night, the fair face, the pleasant mouth, the graceful form in the soft blue cotton gown, made a picture for which an angel might have sat.

Margaret looked at the woman in amazement, and then at the dirty bundle that lay upon the steps at her feet.

"Who are you?" she asked after a moment of silent scrutiny between the two.

"Man come get. Say heap work. Man say big pay."

"O, my brother has been after you. I see. He brought you here this morning before I was awake. That was kind of him. And I thought he was asleep yet."

She was thinking aloud rather than speaking to the woman. Philip, coming around the corner of the house, heard and halted, and his lips settled sternly. A curious expression crossed his face, and then he turned and went back to the other side of the house without being seen. Let her suppose this was the work of her brother if she would. It ought to have been. It was as well she should think so.

But Margaret was grappling with the problem of breakfast, with the addition of this unknown quantity who had come to assist her. Would it be possible for those grimy, greasy hands ever to be clean enough to touch food that was to be eaten by them?

She hit upon the plan, however, of setting the newcomer at some much-needed scrubbing about the doors and windows until they should have breakfast out of the way, and she drew a sigh of relief as she looked about the one living-room and noted how large it was. The woman would not have to be in too close proximity to them while they ate. That was one thing to be thankful for.

She smiled to herself as she hastily laid the table. It was nice of Stephen to go out so early in the morning and get a woman to help. It was dear of Stephen! He was going to justify her utmost ideal of him, she felt sure.

They all felt a strain of embarrassment over them during breakfast. The morning light displayed the crudities of the rude home. Margaret's beauty showed in stronger contrast as she moved about in her dainty blue and white, and seemed some rare bird of paradise dropped into their midst. The two young men in their dark flannel shirts felt ill at ease. They were all facing the problem of what was to be done next.

Margaret felt that the crucial moment for the desire of her heart was coming, and she must walk carefully. She realized, more than did they, the changes it would make in their lives if she remained here as she wished. As for her companions, it seemed to them by the light of morning wisdom an impossibility that she should stay, and they discovered to their own surprise that there was a growing disappointment in their hearts. She had given them a peep into their former lives, and they would turn from it now the more reluctantly.

At last Margaret ventured.

"I don't intend to be a bit of bother when I get settled," she said brightly, "and I will be as patient now as can be; but I would like to know when you think it will be possible for my things to be brought up."

The silence grew impressive. Stephen looked at Philip, and Philip looked into his plate. Margaret watched them anxiously from the corners of her eyes. At last Philip spoke.

"How many things are there?" he asked, merely to make time and give Stephen a chance to tell her what he knew he ought to tell, that this was no place for her to stay.

Margaret would rather her brother had taken the initiative. It was awkward to have to ask favors of a stranger. She wondered how much of a partner he was anyway, and what right he had in the house. Could it be possible that he was part owner? If so, it was more complicated than she had expected.

"O, I'm afraid there are a good many," she answered humbly. "You see I had to bring them or sell them. There wasn't any good place in town to store them where I felt sure they would be safe. It is just a little country town, you know. And some of the things I love. They belonged to my old home. I thought Stephen would like having them about him again, too." She glanced wistfully over at her brother. These old things had been part of the ammunition she had brought with which to fight her battle for the winning of her brother.

"Of course!" said Philip brusquely, scowling across at Stephen. He was disgusted with Stephen for not being more brotherly.

"And there's my piano!" said Margaret, brightening at this slight encouragement. "I couldn't leave that!"

"Certainly not!" said Philip, looking about

at the rough room in a growing wonder of what was coming to it. The impossibility of it all! A piano in the wilderness!

"Great Scott!" ejaculated Stephen, looking up at last, and struggling to express his feelings. "What did you do it for? You can't put a piano and things in here! Think of a piano in this barn!" and he waved his hands eloquently toward the silent, dejected walls.

"O we'll make something besides a barn of it, Stephen," said Margaret, laughing almost hysterically, she was so glad he had spoken at last, even if it was only to attempt a veto to her plans. "I thought it all out this morning when I woke up. This room is lovely, it is so large. It needs a few more windows, perhaps, and a fireplace to make it perfect; but unless you are very much attached to this primitive simplicity you won't know this place after I get it fixed. Just wait till my materials come, and we'll have a real home here. Couldn't you boys build a fireplace, the old-fashioned kind, with a wide chimney in the room? Isn't there any rough stone around here? It would be grand to sit around winter evenings while I read aloud to you, or we all sing. It ought to go right over there!" and she indicated a space between two windows rather far apart, and directly opposite the front door.

"No doubt!" said Philip, looking blankly at the wooden box that now occupied that position and trying to imagine a great stone fireplace in its stead. His fancy failed him, however. He could not see an angel in a bit of rough marble. But the picture of the reading aloud around the open fire on winter evenings, and the music, was alluring.

"Charming," he added, seeing that the weight of the answers all fell upon him. "I never built stone chimneys for a living, but I think I could assist if you would be so good as to direct the job, Miss Halstead. I can't bring my mind to comprehend anything in this room being lovely, but if you say so I suppose it is possible."

"Great Scott!" ejaculated Stephen again in amazement. He was not certain whether Philip was in earnest or not.

"And the piano ought to stand there," said Margaret after the laugh had subsided.

"Certainly," answered Philip again, more amazed than ever. "But might I inquire what you would do with the stove? You couldn't cook on the piano, could you? Or would you expect to use the fireplace?"

The old woman peered in from the window she was washing to see what all the laughter and shouts meant. This seemed to be an exceedingly jolly household into which she had come. She had not heard sounds so light-hearted and merry, so utterly free from the bitter mirth that tinged most of the jollity in this region, in all her life, not since she was a little child and played among the care-free children.

"The stove," said Margaret, "must go into the kitchen, of course."

"Ah!" said Philip meekly. "Strange I didn't think of that. Now, where, might I inquire, is the kitchen?"

Margaret arose and went to the back window, and the two followed her. "It ought to be right here," she said, "and this window should be made into a door leading to it. What is that little square building out there? Can't we have that for a kitchen?"

"That edifice, madam, was originally intended for other purposes, the housing of certain cattle or smaller animals, I forget just what. It isn't of much use for anything. It is in a tumble-down condition. But, if your fairy wand can transform it into a kitchen, so it shall be."

"Say, now that's an idea, Phil!" said Stephen interestedly.

"Then we could use a corner of this room for a dining-room, you know," said Margaret, turning back to the house again. "I have a pretty little cupboard with glass doors that will just fit into that corner, and there are screens and draperies. It will be just charming. I've always wanted to fix up a lovely big room that way. Can't you imagine the firelight playing over the table-cloth and dishes?"

"We haven't seen a table-cloth in so long I'm afraid it would be a strain on our minds to try to do that," said Stephen bitterly. All this talk was alluring, but wholly impossible. Such things could never come into his life. He had long ago given over expecting them. A look of hopeless longing went across his face, and Philip saw and wondered. He had felt that way himself, but somehow it had never seemed to him that his comrade would understand such feelings, he seemed so happy-go-lucky always.

"But what would you do with the roughness of everything?" asked Philip doubtfully. "Pianos and corner cupboards wouldn't like to associate with forests of splinters."

"O, cover them," said Margaret easily, as if she had settled that long ago. "I brought a whole bolt of burlap for such things. It is a lovely leaf-green, and will be just the thing for a background. I don't suppose I have enough; but I can send a sample to New York, and have it here before we need it. I've been thinking this morning what beautiful moulding those smooth, dry corn-stalks would make tacked on next the ceiling. You see, when the walls are covered with something that makes a good background, this will look like a different place."

"You see, Steve, that's what's the matter with you and me. We've never had a suitable background," said Philip slowly.

And thus it was that, amid laughing and questioning, Margaret won her way, and finally saw Philip go off with two horses and a large wagon. She was much troubled that Stephen had not gone with him. It seemed so strange when he was her brother, and Philip would need help, surely, in loading up the furniture. Philip certainly was a queer man. Why did he presume to dictate to Stephen, and, strangest of all, why did Stephen sulkily submit? When she knew her brother better, she would find out, and spur him on to act independently. Again she wondered uneasily whether Philip was not a hindrance to her plans. A man who could so easily command her brother was one whose influence was to be feared.

So Stephen stayed behind, followed his sister about, and did what she asked him to do. In the course of the morning much scrubbing and putting to rights was done, and a savory dinner was under way in spite of the marked absence of needed culinary utensils.

Philip Earle drove away into the sunshine at high speed. He was determined to make all the time he could. He felt uneasy about Stephen, lest he should mount his horse and come after, in spite of injunctions to stay about the house and take care of his sister until they got things into some sort of shape. There were more reasons than one why Philip should be uneasy about Stephen to-day. Nothing must be allowed to happen to startle the newcomer on this her first day. Perhaps she would be able to make things much better. Who knew? It certainly would be great to have something homelike about them. Though it would be all the worse when she would get tired of it,—as of course she would sooner or later,—and take her things and herself off, leaving them to their desolation once more. But Philip would not let himself think of that. With the gayety of a boy of fifteen he called to his horses and hastened over the miles to town.

Margaret and Stephen went out to walk around the house, and plan how the kitchen could be brought near enough for use. Margaret suggested, too, that there ought to be another bedroom built on the other side of the house. She tried to find out how much of a share in things Philip owned, but Stephen was non-committal and morose when she talked of this, and did not seem to take much interest in any changes she would like to make in the house; so she desisted.

She wondered why this was. Could it be that Stephen was short of money? She knew that he had a good sum left to him by his own mother, and her father had also left certain properties which had gone to him at the death of her mother. Could it be that they were tied up so that he could not get at the interest, or was it possible that he had lost some of his money by speculation? Young men were sometimes foolhardy, and perhaps that was it, and he did not like to tell her.

Well, she would just be still on the subjects that she saw he did not wish to talk about, and work her way slowly into his confidence. She had accomplished even more than she had hoped for right at first, for Stephen's letters had not led her to think she would be very welcome, and she had come with a high heart of hope that she might first win his love for herself and then his life for God.

For several years now she had been praying for this stranger brother, until, when she was left in the world alone, she had come to feel that God had a special mission for her with him; and so she had dared to come off here alone and uninvited. She was not going to be daunted by any little thing. She would try to be as wise as a serpent and as harmless as a dove. Meantime she thought she understood Philip Earle somewhat, and she wished that he did not live in the same house with her brother. He might be interesting to try to help, taken by himself; but she was fearful that he would not help her with her brother.

Philip had succeeded beyond his wildest expectations in getting help to bring the freight that he found waiting in the little station. For Margaret had laid her plans well, and, knowing the ways of delays on railroads, had shipped her household goods to this unknown land much in advance of herself, that when she arrived, there might not be so much possibility of sending her away, at least, until she had had opportunity to try her experiment. A girl with a little wider experience of the world, especially of the wild Western world, would not have dared do what she had attempted.

Two stalwart ranchmen Philip enlisted to help him, with their fine team of horses. They were the wildest of the wild men, who drank heavily, and gambled recklessly, and cared not at all that man's days are as grass and he is soon cut off, but took life as if they expected to hold it forever against all odds and have their wicked best from it.

Not a word said Philip about Stephen's sister to them. Something innate made him shrink from speaking of her to them. They were men such as he would not like to have his own sister know. Not that he objected to them himself. They were good fellows in their way. They could tell a story well, though not always of the cleanest sort, and they were fearless in their bravery. But they were men without any moral principles whatever.

Philip, as he drove back home, silent for the most part while the men talked, reflected that his own life was not faultless, and that in the three years that had passed since he came to this country to become a part of it his own moral principles had fallen quite perceptibly. He had not noticed it until to-day, but now he knew it. Somehow the coming of that girl had showed him where he stood. But he still knew what those principles were. And these two men must, if possible, be kept from knowing that Miss Halstead had come.

But how could he manage that? Stephen ought to have been warned. What a fool he was not to have taken Steve out to the barn, and had a good talk with him before he went away, for Steve would never think to be careful. He had no idea of the part he ought to play in the protection of his sister.

The two men had joked him curiously on the amount and kind of furniture they were putting into the wagons, but Philip had only laughed and put them off with other jokes; and in the code of the wild, free life, they accepted for the time, and questioned no more. They knew that when Stephen came he would tell all. Stephen could not keep a thing to himself when he got among his boon companions. They were a trifle curious to know why Stephen did not come along when he expected so important a shipment of goods, and they were exceedingly curious over the piano, feeling sure that either Stephen or

Philip was about to be married and was going to try to keep the matter quiet. But they were obliged to content themselves with Philip's dry answer, "Steve couldn't get away this morning."

Just in sight of the house Stephen came out to meet them, still half-sulky that Philip had insisted on going away alone; and Philip said a few low words to him as he halted the forward wagon, the other two men being together on their own wagon just behind. Stephen demurred, but Philip's insistent tones meant business, he knew, and without waiting to do more than wave a greeting to the two in the other wagon, he walked reluctantly back into the house.

In his heart he was rebelling at Philip and at his sister's presence once more. He could see plainly that it was going to hamper his own movements greatly. His friends were good enough for him, and why should his sister be too good to meet them? If she would stay here, she must take what she found. But he did as Philip told him. He told his sister that he thought she had better go into her room and shut the door until the wagons were unloaded, as they were rough fellows that Philip had brought up with him to help, and she would not want to be about with them. He said it gruffly. He did not relish saying it at all. The men were his especial friends. Had it not been that he knew in his heart that Philip was right, he would not have done it at all.

Margaret wondered, but reluctantly did as he suggested, and went thoughtfully over to the window to look out.

She was right, then. Philip was wild. Stephen knew it. Stephen was trying to help him, perhaps, to reform him or something; and that was why he was so reluctant to speak about Philip's share in the household. And now Philip had brought some of his friends, some rough men that Stephen did not approve and did not wish her to meet, to the house; and he was trying to protect her.

It was dear of Stephen to care for her that way, and she appreciated it, but she felt that it was wholly unnecessary. She felt that her womanhood was sufficient to protect her from insult here in the house of her brother. She was not in the least afraid to be out there and direct where things should go. If Stephen was trying to help Philip to be a better man, then she ought to help, too. It would be another way of helping her brother to help what he was interested in. And these friends of his, could they not be helped, too? It was a pity for Stephen to feel so about it. She wished she had had time to argue with him, for she really ought to be out there to tell them where to place things. It would save a lot of trouble later.

Thus she stood thinking as she heard the stamping of the horses' feet about the front door, the creaking of the wagon-wheels as they ground upon the steps, and then the heavy footsteps, the voices of men, the thuds of heavy weights set down.

She wearied of her imprisonment the more that there was no window in her room from which she could watch operations; and at last, when she heard them discussing the best way of getting the piano out of the wagon, she could stand it no longer. She felt that she was needed, for they had made absurd suggestions, and her piano was very dear to her heart. She must tell them how the piano men in the East always did. It was ridiculous for her to be shut up here, anyway. Stephen might as well learn that now as any time. For an instant she knelt beside the gray cot and lifted a hurried prayer,—just why she knew not, for there was nothing to be afraid of, she was sure,—and then with firm hand she turned the knob of her door, and went out among the boxes and barrels of goods that were all over the room, until she came and stood framed in the sunny doorway, the brilliant noonday glare upon her gold hair and shining full into her dark eyes, her little ruffled sleeve falling away from her white wrist as she raised her hand to shield her eyes.

"Stephen, wait a minute," she called; "I can tell you just how to move that. I watched the men put it in the wagon when it started. It is very easy. You want two rollers. Broomsticks will do."

# 5

## *Margaret's Mission Widens*

THERE was sudden silence outside the front door. The two strangers turned and stared admiringly and undisguisedly. Stephen looked sheepishly triumphant toward Philip, and Philip drew his black brows in a frown of displeasure.

"My sister!" said Stephen airily, recovering himself first, and waving his hand comprehensively toward the two men. He felt rather proud of this new possession of a sister. His own eyes glowed with admiration as he looked at her trim form in its blue and white drapery framed in the rough doorway, one hand shading her eyes, and the animation of interest in her face.

But now Margaret was surprised. Why did Stephen introduce her if he had considered these men too rough for her even to appear in their presence? It was curious. Was he afraid of Philip? Ah! They must be friends of Philip's whom Stephen did not admire, and yet whom he had to introduce on his partner's account, and so he wished to evade it by keeping her out of sight. Well, what mattered it? A mere introduction was nothing. She would let them see by her manner that they were strangers still.

So she acknowledged Stephen's naming of them as "Bennett" and "Byron" with a cool little nod, that only served to increase their admiration. Perhaps the coolness of her manner was to them an added charm. Stephen rose in their estimation, being the possessor of so attractive a sister.

After she had given her wise, clear directions,—which proved to be exceedingly sensible ones, they could not but acknowledge,—she vanished into the house once more, but not, as they supposed, from hearing. She went quickly into Stephen's bedroom, from whose small window she could watch their movements. She intended to see that her directions were carried out and that piano safely landed in the proper place.

Just one short instant she was out of hearing

as she opened the other room door, and closed it softly after her, and drew the torn paper that served as a window-shade slightly aside so that she could see out. During that instant Byron, who was famed among his associates for the terribleness of his oaths and the daring of his remarks, broke forth with a remark to Stephen, prefaced by a fearful oath. The remark was intended to convey the speaker's intense admiration of Stephen's sister, and Stephen himself would have been inclined to take it in the spirit in which it was meant; but Philip, standing close by with darkened countenance, laid a heavy hand on Byron's shoulder, and said in low tones, which yet carried in them a menace, "That kind of talk doesn't go down here!"

It was just then that Margaret's ear became quickened to hear, and her intuition told her that she was the subject of the conversation.

"What's the matter with you, man?" said Byron, shaking off the hand. "Can't you bear to hear a woman praised? Perhaps you'd like a monopoly of her. But she don't belong to you—" with another oath; "and I say it again, Steve; she's a—"

But Philip's hands were at Byron's throat, and the word was smothered before it was uttered.

Margaret dropped the paper shade, and stood back pale and trembling, she knew not why. Was Philip against her? Did he hate to hear her praised even, and did he wish her away, or was he defending her? She could not tell, though there had been something strong and true in the flash of Philip's eye as he sprang toward the other man, that made her fear lest she misjudge him.

What kind of a country was this to which she had come, anyway? And why, if there was need to defend her, had Stephen not been the one to do it, seeing it was Stephen who had warned her to keep away? It was all strange.

She sat thinking, on the hard little cot bed, looking around on the dismal room, and the pity of her brother's life appealed to her more strongly than it had yet done. She resolved to put away any foolish misgivings, and make a home here that should help him to live his life the best that it could be lived. She turned and knelt a minute beside her brother's bed, and asked help of her unseen Guide, a kind of consecration of herself to the mission that had brought her to this strange country.

Then she went once more to the window, and looking out saw the work of unloading the wagons going on as calmly as if nothing had

happened. There was a firmness around Philip's
mouth and chin that was not to be trifled with,
and his eyes seemed to look apart from the
others; but the rest were gayly at work, whistling, calling to one another merrily. Margaret
watched them awhile. The one called Byron
had a handsome face with heavy, dark waving
hair, and big black eyes that were not true, but
were interesting. She shuddered as she remembered the oath he had used to Philip and
Stephen, a much milder one than the first,
which she had not heard. The name of her
Saviour, Jesus Christ! She had never heard it
spoken in that way. It seemed to her the depth
of wickedness. She had not yet dreamed of the
depths to which wickedness can reach.

It rushed over her in a great wave of pity
and sorrow as she watched the muscular arms
lifting her furniture, saw the play of fun and
daring on the handsome features, and thought
that it was the name of his Saviour, as well as
her own, he had used. *His* Saviour, and he did
not know Him, did not recognize, perhaps,
what he was doing. O, if he might be shown!
If she might help to show him! It might be
there would be a way.

And suddenly her mission widened, and
took in Byron, Bennett, Philip, and an un-

known company of like companions; and her heart swelled with the magnitude of the possibility that God might have chosen her to help all these as well as Stephen.

She watched a long time, and listened, too; but there were no more oaths, and no more fights. She studied the faces of the four men as they worked, especially the man who had spoken that awful word, and she prayed as she watched. It was a way that she had been acquiring during her last three or four years of loneliness. And by and by a plan began to open to her mind.

Then she went quietly out to see that the dinner she had started was doing as it should, and prepared to set the table for five instead of three.

By this time some packing-boxes and trunks were where they could be reached, and with Stephen's help she opened one containing some table-linen. It gave her much satisfaction to be able to have a table-cloth the first time she gave a dinner party in her new home.

The goods were all unloaded from the wagons and set under cover, and the two helpers were mopping their perspiring brows, while Philip drove his own wagon to the barn, when Margaret came to the door once more.

"Dinner is ready now," she remarked, quite as if they had all been invited, "and I suppose you would like to wash your hands before you come in. You will find the basin and towels out by the pump at the back door, Mr. Byron and Mr. Bennett." She had watched long enough from the window to know which was which, and she let the slightest glance of her eyes recognize each now, a glance that set them at an immeasurable distance. "And, Stephen, please hurry, because everything will get cold."

Stephen's eyes lit up with pleasure. This was the kind of thing he liked; but it was not what Philip would like, and he knew it. There was no telling but Philip would pitch the two guests out the door and down the hill when he came in and saw them preparing to sit down at the table.

They drew a long and simultaneous whistle when they entered the door together and saw the table draped in snowy white. They were none of them used to table-cloths.

Margaret had cleared a space around the table and arranged boxes for seats where there were not enough chairs; so there was room for all. Before each place she had laid a snowy napkin. To the young fellows so long unused to this necessity of civilization they looked of a dazzling whiteness, and each became immediately conscious of his own poor appearance. She had opened her trunk and found silver knives and forks and spoons, and all were set as she would have set the table in the East for a luncheon of a few friends. She knew no other way. There was enough in this to awe the two wild Western cowboys, who under other circumstances might have proved to be unwelcome guests.

There was a touch of refinement, too, in the few green leaves and blossoms that Margaret had gathered in her morning tour around the house, wild blossoms, it is true, and nothing but weeds in the eyes of the men who daily and unheedingly trod over their like; but here, set in this snowy linen, held in a tiny crystal vase that had also been carefully packed in Margaret's trunk, they took on a new beauty, and were not recognized as belonging to the world in which they lived.

It was like the girl, impulsive and poetical, that she had kept the whole dinner waiting just a minute while she found that vase and added the touch of beauty to the already inviting table. Who knew but the flowers might speak to those men of the God who made them?

And the flowers lifted up their pink, dainty faces, and breathed a silent grace about that board at which they all sat down, creating a kind of embarrassment among the strangely selected company.

It was just as they were sitting down that Philip entered, and paused in the doorway at the sight, his brow darkening.

"Please sit over there, Mr. Earle," said Margaret, passing a plate of steaming soup to the place indicated; and Philip, hesitating, half-reluctant, sat silently down; but his eye ran vividly around the table like the threatening of lightning, in one warning glance.

Philip's look, however, was not needed. The spoons and the napkins and flowers, and above all the young woman, had awed for once the undaunted souls who were noted all about that region for their daring and wickedness. Margaret had rummaged among the tin cans on the shelf of the little cupboard in the corner, and had compounded a most delicious soup with the aid of a jar of beef-extract, a can of baked beans, and another of tomatoes. To be sure, its recipe was not to be found in any cook-book ever published; but it was none the less appreciated for that.

There was half a loaf of baker's stale bread,

which she had toasted and cut into crisp little squares for the soup, and there was corn-meal wherewith she had made a johnny-cake or corn bread of flakiness and deliciousness known only to New England cooks. Not even the old mammies of the South could equal it.

It was not exactly a menu for an Eastern lunch party, but with the aid of another glass of jelly from a box hastily pried open it seemed a feast to the hungry young men who had been their own cooks for long, weary months of famine.

Bennett was tall and lanky, with freckled face, red, straight hair, and white eyelashes heavily shading light-blue eyes. He had a hard, straight mouth, and a scar over his left eye, and was known among his associates as a dead shot. His voice had a hard, cruel ring when he spoke. Margaret did not like his face.

She sat at her end of the table, pouring coffee, or slipping quietly over to the stove, waiting upon their needs, diffusing a softening, silencing influence about the table.

The old woman crept from her duties in the new kitchen which she was scrubbing and purifying, to peep inside the door, and wonder at the strange hush that hovered over the usually hilarious company. She knew the reputation of those young men, and could not understand their silence. Then she looked at the sweet presence of the girl as she presided over the meal, and shook her head, wondering again as she crept silently away.

It was after the last crumb was finished and they had risen from the table,—a mingled look, half of satisfaction in the meal, half of relief that it was over, in their faces,—that Margaret dared her part.

She had made up her mind to do it while she was preparing dinner, and her heart had thumped sometimes so hard that she had scarcely dared try to eat after she had decided upon it. Some rebuke must be given to the man who had uttered the name of Jesus Christ in that awful way. What she should say she did not know. "Lord, give me courage, give me words, give me opportunity!" had been the silent plea during the dinner-time.

And now, as she lifted her brave eyes, stern with the purpose she had in mind, they met the bold, handsome ones of Byron. He was trying to think up something appropriate to say to the hostess for giving them this delight- ful dinner. He was noted for his hilarious speeches; but the usual language in which he framed them would not be according to Philip's ideas, and he did not care to rouse Philip twice in a day. It would scarcely put him into this young woman's good graces to engage in a free fight with Philip Earle before her face.

Something in her troubled gaze embarrassed him as he lounged across the room to where she stood. He was conscious of Philip's forked-lightning glance upon his back, too, as he went; yet he swaggered a little more and held his head higher. He would not be put to shame before a girl. He ran his fingers through his abundant black hair, drew tighter the knotted silk hand-kerchief about his bronzed throat, and came gallantly forward with a few gay words of thanks on his lips, which were unusually free, for him, from profane garnishings.

He even dared to put out his great brown hand to shake hands with her. He had a fancy for holding that little white hand in his.

But Margaret looked at his hand, and then faced him steadily, putting her own hand behind her back.

They did not see Philip, his eyes like a panther's, unconsciously move toward them. Bennett and Stephen drew off by the door to watch what would come.

Her voice was very low, but clear. Philip,

standing behind Byron, could hear every word she said; but the two by the door could not.

"Mr Byron," she said, and there was pain in her voice, "I cannot shake hands with you. You have insulted my best friend."

The red flashed up under the bronze in the young man's cheek, and he drew back as if struck.

He stammered and tried to find words.

It was nothing but a passing word, a flash, he said; Philip and he were as good friends as ever. He did not know, or he would not have spoken. He would apologize to Philip.

Margaret caught her breath. She had not expected to be misunderstood.

"I do not mean Mr. Earle," she answered quietly and steadily; "he is but a new acquaintance. I mean my best friend. I mean Jesus Christ, my Saviour. I heard you speak his name in a dreadful way, Mr. Byron."

She lifted her eyes to his now, and they were full of tears.

The man was dumb before her. What had been a flash of anger and embarrassment grew into shame, deep, overpowering. He had nothing to say. He had never met a thing like this face to face before. It was not something he could point the barrel of his revolver at, nor could he grapple with it and overcome. It was shame, and he had never met real shame before.

The fire in Philip's eyes went out, and he turned half away, as if from something too holy to look upon. He had seen the tears in the girl's eyes, and the real trouble in her voice. Into his own heart Rebuke had sent a shaft as it passed to meet this other man whose guilt was greater.

At last the careless lips, so deserted of all their gay, accustomed words, spoke.

"I did not know—" was all he could say, and he turned and stumbled out of the room, not looking back.

And Margaret, trembling now, with the tears blinding her, took refuge in her room.

## *Margaret Makes a Home*

THE NEXT few days were strenuous ones in the house of the unbidden guest. Philip and Stephen arose early and retired late, and did their regular work at odd times when they could get a chance, while they entered like two boys into the plans of their young commander.

They moved the little cattle-shed near to the house and floored it with some lumber that had been lying idle for some time. They took down the cook-stove, and set it up in the new kitchen, where it soon shone out resplendent in a coat of black under the direction of Margaret and the wondering hand of the old woman.

A box of kitchen utensils which Margaret had considered indispensable to her own career as a housekeeper, and was now thankful she had not left behind, was unpacked, and soon there began to appear on the table wonderful concoctions in the shape of waffles and gems and muffins, which made each meal the rival of the last one, and kept the two young men and the old woman in a continual state of amazement.

Into the midst of all this work came the first Sabbath of Margaret's new life.

A storm had burst in the night, and was carrying all before it, seeming to have made up its mind to stay all day; so there was nothing to do but stay in the house as much as possible.

At the breakfast-table Stephen began to speak of the work they would do that day, and to say what a shame it was raining, as they could not work on a little room to accommodate the old woman, who had now to hobble home at night to her shanty a mile and a half away.

"You forget what day it is, Stephen," said Margaret, smiling. "You couldn't work if it didn't rain. It is Sunday, you know."

Stephen looked up in surprise. He had almost forgotten that Sunday was different from any other day, but he did not wish to confess this to his sister. He drew his brows, scowling, and answered, "O, bother, so it is!"

Then Philip scowled too, but for a different reason, and looked anxiously at the sky to see whether it was really to be a rainy Sunday. He grew suddenly thankful for the rain. But what would he do with Stephen all day?

They were compelled to do some work, after all, for the old woman did not hobble over at all that day, and no wonder: the rain came down in sheets; thunder rumbled; and lightning flashed across the heavens; and Philip blessed the rain again.

"Go into the kitchen, Steve, and wash those dishes," said Philip laughingly, "and I'll help. We're a lazy lot if we can't do the work one day out of seven for our board. It is enough for Miss Halstead to do the cooking." And so they worked together, and Philip hunted around, and managed to make work, little things that Stephen must do at once, and which Margaret kept telling them could wait until the morrow; but Philip insistently kept Stephen helping him at them till dinner was out of the way and it was nearly five o'clock.

The sky was lighting up, and showed some signs of clearing.

Stephen wandered restlessly to the door,

and looked down the road, and then at his watch.

Philip was on the alert, though he did not have that appearance. He glanced at the big piano-case still unopened.

"Miss Halstead," he ventured, "why didn't we open that piano yesterday? If we should knock off a couple of those front boards and get at that keyboard, don't you think you might play for us a little, and while away the rest of this day? Steve will be off to gayer company than ours if you don't amuse him."

He laughed lightly, but there was a troubled something in his voice that caused Margaret to follow his glance toward her brother. She saw the restlessness in his whole attitude, and took alarm. Was it for one or both of the young men she was troubled? She could not have told.

"O, yes, if you can do it easily," said Margaret eagerly. It would be a delight to her to touch the keys of her piano again; it would drive away any lingering homesickness.

Philip's voice again called Stephen's wandering attention, and soon their united efforts brought the row of ivory and black keys into view.

Margaret, seated on a kitchen chair, touched

strong, sweet chords while the two young men settled down to listen.

Sweet Sabbath music she played from memory, a bit from some of the old masters, a page from an oratorio, a strain from the minor of a funeral march, a grand triumphant hymn. Then she touched the keys more softly, and began to sing low and sweetly; and by and by, there came a rich tenor and a grumbling bass from the two listeners as she wandered into familiar hymns that they had sung as little boys.

The rain came on again, and it grew darker, and still they sang, until at last Philip drew a sigh of relief, and realized that it was bedtime and Stephen had not gone to the village. Then Margaret stopped playing, and they all went to get a lunch before retiring.

Margaret, before she slept that night, asked a blessing again on the work she hoped to do, and never dreamed that already she had been used to keep the brother for whose sake she had come this long journey.

After they finished the old woman's room Philip came in with his arms full of great rough stones, and announced that he was ready to begin the fireplace, and he thought it would be best to get the muss and dirt of plaster out of the way before they put things to rights in the living-room.

Margaret had almost forgotten the doubts she had about Philip when she first came, and his strange actions on the morning after her arrival, and was prepared to accept both the young men as good comrades, or brothers. Laughingly they all went to work, Margaret drawing the outline of the fireplace that she thought should be built, and Stephen mixing mortar while Philip brought in stones from a great pile that had been collected by the former owner of the place to build a fence.

"There's nothing like being jack of all trades," said Stephen as he slapped on some mortar with the blade of a broken hoe, and settled into it a great stone that Philip had just brought in.

Margaret's eyes shone as she watched the chimney being built. She saw in her mind's eye a charming room, and she was anxious to get it into shape before another Sabbath, that they might have a quiet, restful time. While she had been playing and singing the night before, there had been revealed to her ways in which she might point the way to her Saviour, and she longed to begin.

There was much to be done in teaching the

strange servant new ways, and in keeping clean
the things they used every day; but Margaret
was one of those whose hands are never idle,
and she had put her whole soul into the
making over of her brother's home; so she
accomplished much in her own way while the
young men worked at masonry and the stone
fireplace grew into comely proportions.

By the time it was finished she had rooted
out from the boxes and barrels most of the
things she would need in the immediate ar-
rangement of this living-room, and had cut and
sewed cushions and fixings ready to put into
place when the time came, so that the work of
refurnishing went rapidly forward. Indeed, the
two helpers became fully as eager to see the
room finished as was the young architect.

Margaret had bought a number of things
before she left the East that she thought she
would be likely to need in arranging her own
room, which she wanted to make as pretty as
possible to keep her from getting homesick. All
this plan she now abandoned, and set herself to
put these pretty things into the adornment of
the great, bare living-room which she meant
should be the scene of her labors.

Among other things there were bright materials for cushions, and there were rolls of

paper enough to hang the walls of a reasonably large room. A careful calculation and much measurement soon made it evident that this paper would cover the most of the walls of this room, which was the size of an ordinary whole house without any partitions. She puzzled a while to know whether she should risk sending for more, but finally a bright idea occurred to her as she looked at the large bundle of green burlap that was lying in the box with the paper. This she had intended for draperies, or floor covering, if necessary, or maybe covering for a chest or a cushion. Now all was plain before her.

The paper had an ivory ground on which seemed to be growing great palms as if a myriad of hothouses had let forth their glories of greenery. There was enough of this paper to cover the two sides and front of the room. That was delightful. It would look as if the room opened on three sides into a palm grove. On the back end, in the centre of which was the great stone fireplace, she would put the plain moss-green burlap, fastened along its breadths with brass tacks. Two or three good coats of whitewash would give the ceiling a creamy tint, and she could cut out a few of the palms from the paper to apply in a dainty design in the centre and corners.

The two young men looked bewildered when she tried to explain, and she finally desisted, and issued her directions.

They covered the back of the room first; and, when the mossy breadths were smoothly on over the rough boards, fastened at intervals with the gleaming tacks, the old stone fireplace stood out finely against the dark background.

"Now, if you have any guns and things, that is the place to put them," said Margaret, pointing to the wall about the fireplace, and Philip proudly brought out a couple of guns, and crossed them on the wall to the right, while Stephen fastened a pair of buffalo-horns over the door to the left that led into the new kitchen. This side of the room was at once denominated the dining-room, and Margaret unwrapped a handsome four-panel screen of unusual size, wrought in black and gold, and stood it across that corner.

They turned with avidity to follow her next directions, having more faith in the result than they had before. And another day or two saw the walls papered and the ceiling smiling white with its green traceries here and there.

It did not take long after that to unpack rugs and furniture. Margaret had brought many things from the old home, rare mahogany furniture and Oriental rugs, that a wiser person might have advised her to leave behind until she was sure of making a home in this far land. But the girl rejoiced in the beauty of the things she had to give to her "life-work," as she pleased to call it, and had brought everything with her that she intended to keep at all.

The rough old floor with its wide cracks and unoiled boards did not look so bad when they were almost covered with a great, soft rug of rich, dark coloring, and set off here and there by the skin of a tiger or a black bear, or by a strip of white goat-skin.

A wide, low seat, covered with green and piled with bright cushions, ran along the wall to the right of the fireplace. In the corner beyond the window was a low bookcase, which Margaret had intended for her own room, and again beyond her bedroom door another low bookcase ran along to the other bedroom door. These doors were hidden by dark-green curtains of soft, velvety material: and no one would have suspected the rough, cheap doors behind them. By each one there stood on the top of the bookcase, half against the green of the curtain and half mingling with the lifelike palms on the wall, a living palm in a terra-cotta jardinière, which made the pictured ones but seem more real.

The piano stood near the front of the room, across the right-hand corner; and a wide, low couch invited one to rest and listen to the music.

The rest of the room that was not dining-room was filled with easy chairs, a large, round mahogany table with a most delightful reading-lamp in the middle, and more books, while Stephen's old writing-desk stood across the left-hand front corner.

It was all most charming to look upon, this finished room, when the weary workers at last sat down to a belated supper Saturday evening, and realized what they had accomplished during the week.

There was much to be done yet. Margaret, as she ate her supper, glanced around, and planned for a row of little brass hooks against the wall, whereon should hang her tiny tea-cups, and wondered how she should manage a plate-rail for the saucers, in this country without mouldings. The little glass-faced buffet that was to hold the china still stood on the floor in the corner, waiting its turn to be hung, and the pictures were as yet unpacked; but there was time enough for that. There was a room in which to spend the Sabbath, and she prayed that her work might now begin.

Softly there crept up through the darkness of the sky the dawn of another Sabbath day, and Margaret arose with eager anticipations. In the first place, she meant to make Stephen, and Philip, too, if possible, go with her to church. That, of course, was the right place in which to begin the Sabbath.

Before she left her room she laid out upon her bed the things she would wear to church, choosing them with care that she might be neatly and sweetly attired in the house of the Lord, and that she might be as winsome as possible to those she wished to influence.

She did not acknowledge even to herself that she had some doubt in her mind as to whether she should accomplish making Stephen and Philip attend church, for she meant to accomplish that in spite of all obstacles.

Nevertheless, she went about her self-set task with great care and deliberation, prefacing her request with the daintiest breakfast with which they had yet been favored.

It was just as they finished that she brought forward the subject that was so near to her heart and about which she had been praying all the morning.

"Stephen, what time do we have to start for church? Is it far from here? You don't go on horseback, do you?"

Stephen dropped his knife and fork on his plate with a clatter, and sat back in astonishment; and there was a blank silence in the room for some seconds.

## "Brothers No Good"

"TO church!" Stephen uttered the words half mockingly. "What time do we start! Well, now, Phil, how far should you say it was to the nearest church?"

A mirthless laugh broke from Philip. It was involuntary. A wave of bitterness rolled over him as a wave of the ocean higher than the others might break over the head of one who was bravely trying to breast the tide. As soon as he had uttered the laugh he was sorry, for he felt the shock this would be to Margaret even before he saw her start at his harsh laughter.

These two young men were alike in the bitterness that each carried in his heart, but Stephen's had been caused by the hardness of his heart toward his earthly father, while Philip had hardened his heart, for what he considered just cause, toward his Father in heaven; and of the two his bitterness was the more galling.

Philip checked the laugh, which had really been but the semblance of one, and answered steadily with his eyes on his plate, "About forty miles by the nearest way, I should judge."

Stephen's eyes were twinkling with fun as he tipped his chair back against the wall and watched his sister. He had no inkling of the desolation this would bring to her, and he could not understand, perhaps did not notice, the whiteness of her face as she looked at him, only half comprehending. It was given to Philip, the stranger, to feel with her the appalling emptiness of a country without a church. Dismay dropped about her as a garment.

"But what do you do?" she faltered. "Where do you go to service on Sunday?"

"Same as any other day," laughed Stephen carelessly. "'The groves were God's first temples,'" he quoted piously; "suppose we go out in search of one. This will be a first-rate day for your first lesson in riding horseback. It won't do for you to stick in the house at work all the time."

But Margaret's face was flushed and troubled.

"Do you mean you don't go anywhere to church?" she asked pathetically. "Is there no service in the town? Are there no missionaries even, out here?"

"There isn't even a town worth speaking of, Miss Halstead," answered Philip, feeling that some one must answer her earnestly. "You do not know what a God-forsaken country you have come to. Churches and missionaries would not flourish here if they came. You will not find it a pleasant place to stay. Men get used to it, but women find it hard."

She lifted her troubled eyes to his, wondering in an underthought whether he was hinting that she should go back where she came from; but she saw in his kind face no eagerness to get rid of her, as his eyes met hers. She turned sadly toward the window, looking out on the stretch of level country away down the hill, thinking with despair of the place to which she had come and the hopelessness of carrying out her plans without the aid of a church and a minister.

She had thought her part would be simply to make a good home for her brother, to speak a quiet word when opportunity offered, and to use her influence to put him under the power of the gospel. But out here it seemed there was no gospel, unless she preached it. For this she was not prepared.

Perplexed and baffled, she hardly knew with what words she declined her brother's urgent request to go riding with him, to which were added the most earnest solicitations of his partner when he saw that Stephen was not going to succeed. She wondered afterwards at the anxiety and annoyance in Philip's eyes when she told him firmly that she did not ride on Sunday, and would rather stay quietly at home. It seemed strange to her that he should try to interfere between her and her brother. Then she went into her little log room and shut the door, and knelt in disheartened prayer beside her bed. Had she, then, come out on a fruitless mission? For what would it avail if she did bring palm-covered walls and pianos and books into her brother's life, if there were no means by which he could be brought to see the love of the Lord Jesus Christ?

She was scarcely roused from her disappointed petitions by the sound of a rider leaving the dooryard. She wondered idly whether it were Philip, but soon she heard another horse's quick tread, and, going to the window, was just in time to see Philip fling himself upon his horse and ride at a furious pace off down the road.

Quiet settled down upon the house, and Margaret realized with disappointment that both the young men had gone away. Why had she not tried to keep Stephen with her? Perhaps he would have listened to her while she read something, or she might have sung. Philip, it was quite evident, had intended going off all the time, and was only anxious to get her and Stephen out of the way so that he could do as he pleased. The tears came into her eyes, and fell thick and fast. How ignominiously had she failed! Even the little she might have done she had let slip by because of her disappointment that God had not arranged things according to her expectations. Perhaps it might have been better for her even to go on the ride with Stephen rather than for him to go off with some friends who never had a thought of God or His holy day.

Thus reflecting, she read herself some bitter lessons. She had forgotten to ask for the Spirit's guidance, and had been going in her own strength; or she might have been shown a better way and been blessed in her efforts.

By and by she went out where the old woman sat outside the kitchen door, mumbling and glowering at the sun-clad landscape. Perhaps she might essay a humble effort with this poor creature for a Sabbath-day sacrifice.

"Marna, do you know God?" she asked, sitting down beside the old woman and speaking tenderly.

The woman looked at her curiously, and shook her head.

"God never come at here," she answered. "Missie, you—*you* know God?"

"Yes," answered Margaret earnestly. "God is my Father."

"God your Father! No. You not come off here; you stay where you Father at. God, you Father, angry with you?"

"No, my Father loves me. He sent His Son to die for me. God is your Father, too, Marna."

The old woman shook her head decidedly.

"Marna have no father. Fathers all bad. Fathers no love anybody but selves. Brothers no much good, too. All go off, leave. All drink. I say, stay 'way. No come back drunk. Knock! scold! hate! I say stay 'way. Drink self dead!"

Marna was gesticulating wildly to make up for her lack of words. Suddenly she turned earnestly to the girl, with a gleam of something like motherliness in her wrinkled, wicked old face.

"What for Missie come way here? Brothers no good. All go own way. Make cry!" and Marna's work-worn finger traced down the delicate cheek, which was still flushed with the recently shed tears.

Margaret instinctively drew back, but she did not wish to hurt the old woman's feelings; so she answered in as bright a tone as she could summon.

"Brothers are not all bad, Marna. Some are good. My brother was lonely here, and I came to take care of him."

"'Take care! Take care!'" muttered the old woman. "And who 'take care' of Missie? Men go off, stay all day. Drink. Come home drunk! Ach! No, no, Missie go back. Missie go off while men gone. Not see brothers any more."

Margaret was half frightened over this harangue; but she tried to be brave and answer the poor creature, though her heart misgave her as a great fear began to rise.

"No, Marna," she said smiling through her fear; "I cannot go back. God sent me, and until He tells me to go back I cannot go."

"God love you and send you here? Then He never come here. He don't know—"

"Yes, He knows, Marna, and He is here, too," she answered softly, as if reassuring herself. "Listen!"

And Margaret began at the beginning of the story of the cross, and told it all to the wondering old woman as simply as she knew how. But, when she had finished, the listener only shook her head, and murmured:

"No, God never love Marna. Marna have bad heart. No love for good in heart. No heavenly Father love."

It was time to get dinner ready, and Margaret arose with a sigh, a great depression settling on her heart. Not even to this poor old woman could she show the light of Christ.

She gave herself to the preparations for the noon-day meal for a little while, thinking soon to hear the sound of horses coming up the road; but, though the dinner got itself done and sent forth savory odors on the air, and Margaret stood with anxious, wistful eyes shaded with a hand that had grown strangely cold with a new fear, there came no sound of horses.

The girl ate a few mouthfuls, and had the dinner put away. The old woman went about muttering:

"Men no come. Men off. Have good time. Missie cry. Missie go home. Not stay."

The stars came out thickly like sky-blossoms unfolding all at once, and the sky drew close about the earth; but still there came no sound of travellers along the long, dark road.

Margaret went in at last from her vigil on the door-step and lit the great lamp. It was a disappointing Sabbath. It was more than that; it seemed a wasted Sabbath. She might much better have been riding with Stephen if perchance she might have said some helpful thing to him. And the old woman rocking and muttering to herself in the back doorway, what good had she done to her?

At last she could bear the silence and her fears no longer.

She called to Marna to come in. "Sit down," she said gently. "I will sing to you about Jesus."

Marna sat down with folded hands on a little wooden stool, and listened while Margaret sang.

She chose the songs that were in simple language, that told of Jesus and His love; songs that spoke to weary, burdened ones and bade them rest; songs that told of forgiveness and a Father's love.

A long time she sang; and then, yearning for a help, she knew not what, feeling as if she must have a companionship in her need, she came over to the old woman, took her hand, and drew her down beside the fireplace seat.

"Come," said she. "We will talk to God."

Wonderingly, half fearfully, the old woman knelt, watching the girl with wide-open eyes the while; and Margaret closed her eyes, and said:

"O God, show Marna how her Father loves her. Make Marna love God. Make Marna good, for Jesus' sake."

As under a spell the old woman stood up; her eyes half frightened, half fascinated, were upon the girl's face.

Margaret smiled and said good-night, but Marna went out under the stars, and muttered wonderingly, "Make Marna good?" as if it were a thing that had to be and she could not see how it could be.

Then Margaret locked the door, and turned out the light, and sat down at the window to watch and pray. During that time there was revealed to her a part of what she might do in this land without a God or a temple. Out of her darkness, her fear, and her feebleness came a strength not her own.

It must have been long past midnight—her watch had run down and she could not tell—

when at last faint sounds came slowly up the hill; and silently, slowly there crept past her window and wound around the house to the barn two horsemen, strangely close together. One seemed to be supporting the other. They spoke no word; but one of them turned his head as he passed her window, and looked, though she could not tell which one it was.

Neither of them came to the house that night, though she lighted the lamp and waited awhile for them. She concluded they did not wish to disturb her.

Then, not caring to take off her clothes, she lay down and wept. After all the long, hard day the tension was loosened at last, but what yet did she know? Was one of her new-found fears dissipated? Was she sure that Stephen had come home with Philip, and was now in the barn lying in the hay? Was she sure that it had been Philip? They might have been two tramps—but no. Tramps would not come to a desolate land like this. They would tramp to more profitable places for plying their beggarly trade. Somehow for herself a strange peace settled down upon her. She was not afraid that anything would happen to her. She feared only for her brother—and—yes, she must admit it—for his friend. For, after all, he was her brother too, in a larger, broader sense, but still the son of her heavenly Father.

And those words of Marna's, what had they meant? Did the two with whom she had come to make her home, drink? And, if so, how could she ever hope to help and save them, just she alone in that country without a church? For the absence of a Christian church and a Christian minister seemed to leave her most inexpressibly alone.

And yet not alone, for out of the darkness of her room came the words to her heart, "And lo, I am with you alway."

Then she prayed as she had never prayed before, prayed until her soul seemed drawn up to meet the loving Comforter, Strengthener, and Guide. In that consecration hour she laid down herself, her fears and wishes, and agreed to do what God would have her do here in this lonely place, against such fearful odds as might be; herself alone with God.

Out in the hay lay Philip, body and mind weary with the fight of the day, in which he had not won, yet too troubled to sleep now that he had the chance.

With anxious eyes he peered through the darkness toward the house, and wondered how it had fared with the one who had waited all day while he had been in the forefront of battle. Was she frightened at being left so late alone? Had she seen them when they came in? Had she guessed at all what the trouble was, or had she coupled them both in deserting her? Philip's heart was very bitter to-night, and against God. He felt like cursing a God who would let a woman, and so fair a woman, suffer. Poor, straying child of God, who knew not the comfort of trusting and leaning on the everlasting arm; who knew not that even suffering may bring a beauteous reward!

8

## *A Vexatious Proposal*

STEPHEN slept late the next morning; and, when he came heavy-eyed and cross to the breakfast-table, he complained of a headache. But Philip sat silent, with grave lines drawn about forehead and mouth. He was too strong a man to show the signs of fatigue or loss of sleep in any other way.

Margaret had come out from the horror of the night with peace upon her brow, but her eyes looked heavy with lack of sleep. Philip gave her one long look while she was pouring the coffee, and saw this. It angered him to think she had suffered.

Margaret was sweetness itself to her brother. She insisted upon his lying down on the long seat by the chimney, while she shaded his eyes from the glare of the morning, and brought a little chair near by, and read to him. When he turned his head away from her entirely because for very shame he could not face this kindness, and know what in his heart he really was, she laid the book aside, and, bringing a bowl of water, dipped her cool, soft hand in it, and made passes back and forth across the temples that really throbbed in earnest.

Something was working in his easily stirred heart, something that went beyond the mere surface where most emotions were born and died, with him; and, as her hand went steadily back and forth with that sustained motion that is so comforting to sick nerves, he reached up a shaking hand, and caught hers, and his voice choked as he said,

"You are a good girl,—a good sister!"

Then Margaret stooped over, and kissed his lips, and murmured softly, "Dear brother, now go to sleep; and, when you wake up, you will feel better."

Stephen had much ado to keep back the moisture that kept creeping to his eyelids with stinging, smarting stealth; and he was glad when she finally thought him asleep and tiptoed away. Not for long years had he felt a lump like that that was now growing in his throat till it seemed it would burst. But by and by the quiet and the darkness brought sleep; and Philip, looking anxiously in, went out quickly with a relieved sigh.

The dinner was late that day, for Stephen slept long, and Margaret would not have him disturbed. But when it came it was delicious. Strong soup seasoned just right, home-made bread, delicious coffee, and a quivering mound of raspberry jelly, cool and luscious with the flavor of raspberries from the old New England preserve-closet. It was marvellous how many things this sister could make from canned goods and boxes of gelatine. There seemed to be no end to the variety.

But Stephen was restless as the dinner neared its close, and Philip looked anxiously toward him.

Stephen shoved his chair back with a creak on the floor, and said crossly that he believed he would ride down to the village for the mail. He needed to get outdoors; it would do his head good. Philip frowned deeply, and set his lips for a reply; but before he could speak Margaret's sweet voice broke in eagerly.

"O, then, give me my lesson in riding, Stephen, please. It is a lovely afternoon, and will soon be cool. I don't want to be left behind again. I was sorry I had not gone with you yesterday. Please do; I am in a great hurry to learn to ride so I can go all about and see this country."

Philip's face relaxed. He waited to see what Stephen would do, and after a bit of coaxing Stephen consented, although Philip felt uneasy yet.

The horses were saddled and brought to the door, and Philip held the bridle of the gentler horse while Stephen helped his sister to mount, giving elaborate advice about how to hold the reins and how to sit. Then they were off.

"Go the east road, Steve!" called Philip as they rode away from him; but Stephen drew his head up haughtily, and did not answer. Then Philip knew he had made a mistake, and he bit his lip as he turned quickly toward the barn. There was still another horse on the place, though it was not a good riding-horse, and had some disagreeable habits, which left it free generally to stay behind when there was any pleasure riding to be done. Philip flung his own saddle across her back now, and, hardly waiting to pull the girths tight, sprang into it and away after the two, who were turning westward, as he had been sure Stephen would do after his unfortunate remark.

He urged the reluctant old horse into a

smart trot, and soon caught up with the riders, calling pleasantly:

"Made up my mind I would come along too. It was lonely staying behind by myself."

Stephen's only answer was a frown. He knew what Philip meant by following. His anger was roused at Philip's constant care for him. Did Philip think him a fool that he couldn't take care of himself with his sister along?

Margaret, too, was a little disappointed. She had hoped to get nearer to her brother during this ride, and perhaps to find out where he had been the day before, and have a real heart-to-heart talk with him. But now here was this third presence that was always between her and her brother, and hindered the talk.

Philip, however, was exceedingly unobtrusive. He rode behind them or galloped on before, dismounting to gather a flaming bunch of flowers, and riding up to fasten them in the bridle of the lady's horse, and then riding on again. Stephen ignored him utterly, and Philip gayly ignored the fact that he was ignored. Margaret came to feel his presence not troublesome, and in fact rather pleasant, hovering about like a guardian angel. Then she laughed to herself to think of her using that simile. To think of an angel in a flannel shirt, buckskins, and a sombrero!

It was Philip's quiet hint—no, not a hint, merely a suggestion that a certain turn would bring them to a view of the river—that caused Margaret to plead for going that way just as they had come to a critical turn in the road. Stephen, all unsuspecting, turned willingly, thinking they would go back soon and find their way to the village; but wary Philip tolled them on still further until the town with its dangers was far behind them. Then Stephen awoke to the plot that had been laid for him, and rode his horse sulkily home; but the deadly fiend that slumbered within him was allayed for the time, and he went to his room and slept soundly that night.

There was plenty of work to be done yet upon the house. Philip surprised them all a few days later by driving up to the door before breakfast with a load of logs, several men and another load of logs following after him. The sound of the axe, saw, and hammer rang through the air that day, and by night a good-sized addition of logs, divided into two nice rooms, was added to the right-hand side of the living-room.

Margaret's eyes shone. It was just the addition she had spoken of to Stephen, to which he had seemed so opposed. Her heart swelled with gratitude toward him. It seemed she did not yet understand this brother, who was sometimes so cold, but who yet was trying to do all in his power to please her. She watched the work some of the time, and was surprised to find that, while Stephen worked with the rest, he yet took all his orders from Philip as did the others, and seemed to expect Philip to command the whole affair. It was still more strange that all the orders were just what she had suggested to Stephen on the first walk around the house.

It was as they were coming to the supper-table that evening that she attempted to tell her brother how good it was of him to do all these things that she suggested. She thought they were alone; but Philip had come in behind them while they were talking, and Stephen saw him. The back of Stephen's neck grew red, and the color stole up around his golden hair as he said laughingly:

"O, thank Phil for that. He's the boss carpenter. I couldn't build a house if I had to stay out in the rain the rest of my life."

Margaret looked up brightly, and gave Philip the first really warm smile he had received from her, a smile that included him in the family circle.

"I will thank him, too," she said and put out her hand to grasp his large one, rough with the handling of many logs. But she left her other hand lovingly on her brother's shoulder, and Stephen knew she had not taken back the gratitude she had given him. It somehow made him feel strangely uncomfortable.

In a few days the addition to the house was in good order and the windows draped in soft, sheer muslin.

There seemed to be good cheer everywhere. The three householders took a final survey of the premises before the sun went down.

"If we could only grow bark on the outside of the old boards on the main part of the house!" said Margaret wistfully.

"Nothing easier," answered Philip quickly. "It shall be done."

"What do you mean?" asked Margaret.

"Why, cover it with bark," answered Philip. "Steve, get up early with me in the morning, and we'll strip enough bark down in the ravine to cover one side of this front before breakfast."

"Won't that be beautiful?" said Margaret,

clapping her hands childishly, and the stern lines in Philip's face broke into a pleased smile. He was glad he had suggested it. What was it about this girl that always made one feel glad when he had done her a favor? Other girls he had known had not been that way.

That night he slept in the house for the first time since Margaret came to live there. The front room of the addition was fitted up for him. Margaret had just found out that his only bed had been in the hay, and that he had permanently and quietly given up his room to her. She had supposed before that there was a room over the barn, large and comfortable, which he called his own, though she had indeed thought little about it. She took especial pains with the furnishing of Philip's room. She felt it was due to him for turning out of his own for her. It was not difficult to make it beautiful. There was enough fine old mahogany furniture left. She picked out the handsomest things, and arranged them attractively. She had not yet fixed up her own room further than to have her own bedstead set up in preference to the hard little cot, but she wanted to make Philip's as attractive as possible.

As a final touch she went to her room, and unpinned from her wall the photograph of the sweet-faced woman with the white hair, and, framing it in a little leather case of her own, set it upon the white cover of Philip's bureau. And it was his mother's eyes that looked at Philip in the morning as he opened them for the first time in his new abode. He lay for a moment, looking at the picture, wondering how it got there, blessing the thoughtfulness that had so placed it, wondering what his mother would think of him now in this strange, wild life. Wondering, too, what she would think of the girl who was bringing to pass in this desolate house such miracles of change. He touched the smoothness of the sheet and the pillow-case, and realized that he had missed such things as these for a long time, and had not known it.

Those were busy, happy days. At times Stephen seemed to be wrought up to the same pitch of enthusiasm and violent effort that kept the other two at work. He did not seem to want to stop for his meals even, until all was finished. And one night, when they were standing off, looking at the almost completed outside of the house, he said,

"We ought to have a housewarming when it gets done."

"Certainly," said Margaret. "We will do it

by all means. How soon can we have it, and whom will you invite?"

But, as she turned to go into the house, she caught that look of disapproval on Philip's face, the look she had not seen for several days, and wondered at it.

"Let's have it next Sunday," said Stephen enthusiastically. "It's getting cooler weather now, and by evening we can have a fire in that jolly new fireplace of Phil's. And we'll ask all the fellows, of course."

Philip stood still, aghast. If Margaret had not been there, he would have fairly thundered. But his tongue was tied. This must be managed, if possible, without letting her know what a precipice she was treading near. She would be overcome if she knew all.

"Is there no other day but Sunday, Stephen, dear?" asked Margaret, and her troubled voice was very soft and pleading. "You know I always make the Sabbath a holy day and not a holiday. I would much, *much* rather have it some other time."

She did not say no decidedly to his proposition, remembering her Sunday's experience when she had declined to ride with him. Perhaps there was some way out of the perplexity better than that. She would not antagonize her brother yet, and she would ask her Guide. There surely would be a way.

"No, there isn't any other time when they all can come," answered Stephen shortly. "But of course if you have your puritanical notions, I suppose it's no use. I can't see what harm it would do for the boys to be here that day more than any other day. You can go off into your room, and pray if you want to; and the boys won't be doing any worse than they would do down in the village carousing round."

Stephen was angry, and was forgetting himself. Philip's cheeks flamed with indignant pity for the girl who winced under her brother's words.

"O, Stephen, *don't,* please! Let me think about it. I want to do what you wish if there is a right way." She spoke pleadingly. There were tears in her voice, but her eyes were bright and dry.

"Well, then, do it," said Stephen sulkily. "It won't hurt your Sabbath to give us some tunes on the piano. The boys will like that better than anything else. They don't hear music out here."

Margaret looked up troubled, but thoughtful.

"I'll think about it to-night, Stephen, and

tell you in the morning. Will that do? I'll really try to see if I can please you."

Stephen assented sulkily. He had very little idea she would do it. He remembered her face that Sunday when she declined to ride with him. He set her down as bound by prejudices and of very little use in such a country as that.

But Philip, troubled, hovered about the door.

"Miss Halstead," he called pretty soon, "the moon is rising; have you noticed how bright the stars are? Come out and look at them."

"Come, Stephen," said Margaret.

"What do I care for the stars?" said Stephen sulkily, and he went into his room and shut the door.

Margaret's eyes were filled with tears; but she winked them back, and came to the door, anxious to get to the kindly starlight that would not show her discomfiture.

"Miss Halstead, I beg you will not think of doing what Steve asks," said Philip low and earnestly.

"Why not, Mr. Earle? Have you any conscientious scruples against company on Sunday?" Her voice was cold and searching.

"No, of course not," said Philip impatiently.

"Then why? You spent all day one Sunday

off somewhere, presumably on a pleasure excursion."

"It was anything but a pleasure excursion, Miss Halstead," said Philip, his face growing dark with anger in the starlight. "But that has nothing whatever to do with the matter. I beg you will not do this for your own sake. You do not know what those fellows are. They will not be congenial to you in the least."

"Does that make any difference if they are my brother's friends?" Margaret drew herself up haughtily. "I thank you for your advice, Mr. Earle; but this is my brother's house, and of course I cannot stop his having guests if he wishes. I do not like company on Sunday; but, if they must come, I shall do my best to make it a good Sunday for them. More than that I cannot promise. Do you think I can?"

There was a mixture of coldness and pleading in her voice which would have been amusing at another time. But she had silenced Philip most effectually. He bit his lips, and turned away from the house to walk out into the starlight with his vexation.

9

## *A Ride and a Rescue*

MARGARET slept but little that night. A great plan had come to her, born of anxiety and prayer. At first she thought it seemed preposterous, impossible! She drew back, caught her breath, and prayed again; but over and over the idea recurred to her.

It was this. Perhaps God had sent her out here into these wilds to witness for Himself, yes, even among rough men like the two that had taken dinner with them that first day after her arrival.

Could she do it? Could she make that proposed Sunday gathering into a sanctified, holy thing? She, who had never spoken in public in her life, except to read a low-voiced essay from a school platform? She, who had always shrunk from doing anything publicly, and let honors pass her rather than make herself prominent? She who had never been taught in ways of Christian work, other than by her own loving heart?

Could she do it?

And *how* could she do it?

The utmost she knew about Christian work was learned in the class of boys she had taught in Sunday school at home. But they had been boys, most of them still in knee-trousers, and under home discipline. They had loved her, it is true, and listened respectfully to her earnest teaching. Even their mischief had given way before her hearty, trusting smile. They had learned their lessons, and thought it no disgrace to answer her questions. They had come to her home occasionally, and seemed to enjoy it, and she had talked with several of them about holy things. Two she had labored with and knelt beside while she heard their first stumbling acknowledgment that God was their Father and Jesus Christ their Saviour.

But this was all very different from bringing the gospel to a lot of men who knew little and cared less about God or their own salvation. She shuddered in the dark as she remembered the sound of that awful oath that Byron had let fall. How could she do it? Was it right and modest for her to try?

Then out of the night she seemed to feel her Saviour's eyes upon her, and to know that such things must not count against the great need of souls when she was the only one at hand to succor. And she bowed her head, and answered aloud in a clear voice,

"I will do what you want me to do, Jesus; only let me help save my brother."

The sleeper in the next room stirred, and started awake at the unusual sounds, and thought over the words he had heard, trying to put a meaning to them, but thought he had dreamed; so he slept again, uneasily.

After Margaret had said, "I will," to her Master the rest came easily. The plan, if it was a plan, was His. The Spirit would guide her. She had asked for such guidance. If it was of God, it would be crowned with some sort of success. She would be made to understand that it was right. If it was her own faulty waywardness, it would fail. It surely could do no harm to try to have a Sunday-school class of any of Stephen's friends who would come; and, if they refused or laughed at her, why, then she could sing. The gospel could always be sung, where no one would listen to it in other form. It would be a question of winning her brother over, and that might be difficult.

Stay! Why need she tell him? Why not take them all by guile, and make the afternoon so delightful to them that they would want to come again? Could she?

Her breath came quickly as the idea began to assume practical proportions and she perceived that she was really going to carry it out. She had ever a spirit of strong convictions and impulsive fancies; else she would have stopped right here. But perhaps in saying that too little weight is given to the fact that she had given herself up to the guidance of One wiser than herself.

Just before the stars paled in the eastern sky she lay down to rest, her mind made up, and her heart at peace. As for Philip's words of warning, she had forgotten them entirely. Philip she did not understand, but neither did he understand her.

The two young men were both surprised the next morning when she told them, quietly enough, that she would be glad to help them entertain their friends on Sunday afternoon, provided they would allow her to carry out her own plans. She thought she could promise them a pleasant time, and would they trust her for the rest?

It was very sweetly said, and her dainty morning gown, a touch of sea-shell pink in it this time that made her look like an arbutus blossom in the greenery of the room, sat about her so trimly that her brother could but admire her as he watched her put the sugar into his coffee.

It must be admitted that Stephen was surprised, but he was too gay himself to realize fully the depth of earnestness in any one else; so he concluded that Margaret had decided to let her long-faced ideas go, and have a good time while she was here; and he resolved to help her on with it. She was certainly a beauty. He was glad she had come.

But Philip's face darkened, and the little he ate was quickly despatched. After that he excused himself, and went out to the barn. He was angry with Margaret, and he was troubled for her. He knew better than she what she was bringing upon herself; moreover, her brother, who should have been a better protector of so precious a sister, knew even better than he. Why did not Stephen see, and stop it?

But Philip foresaw that matters had gone too far for it to be wise in him to say a word to Stephen. Former experience had taught him that Stephen took refuge from pointed attacks in flight to his companions in the village, which always ended in something worse.

Philip was so angry that after he had done all the work about the barn-yard that was ready for him he concluded to take himself away for a while. There was enough in the house to keep Stephen busy and interested for the day. The fear that had made him keep guard ever since the arrival of Margaret Halstead was for the time dominated by his anger at both brother and sister; and he took his revenge in going off across the country many miles on a piece of business connected with a sale of cattle which he had proposed to make for some time, but had put off from week to week.

He did not stop to explain to the household except in a sentence or two, and then he was off. Margaret noticed the hauteur in his tones as he announced his departure at the door, but so full was she of her plans for Sunday that she took little heed of it. It did not matter much about Philip anyway. He was only an outsider, and, besides, he would feel differently, perhaps, when Sunday came.

Philip's anger boiled within him, and grew higher and hotter as he put the miles between himself and the cause of it. He wished himself out of this heathenish land, and back into civilization. He decided to let people take care of themselves after this. Of what use was it to try to save this girl from a knowledge of her brother's true self? She was bound to find it out sooner or later, and she would perhaps only hate him for his effort.

But Stephen, after teasing his sister to discover what plan she had for the entertainment of their guests, made up his mind to make the most of Philip's absence, and get his guests well invited before that autocrat interfered. It was marvellous that he had not done so already. Therefore he slipped away to saddle his horse while his sister was busy in her room, and, only leaving a message with Marna, rode away into the sunlight, as gay of heart as the little insects that buzzed about his horse, and with less care for the morrow than they had.

Margaret was disappointed to find her brother gone when she presently came out, for she had planned to get him to do several little things about the house that morning, and while he was doing them she had intended to sound him on the friends he would invite. She wondered whether there were many and whether among them there would be any who could help her in the work of establishing her Sunday school. There must be some good women about there. Surely she could get a helper somewhere.

But perhaps this first time it would be only two or three of Stephen's best friends. He had spoken of "the fellows," and it would be better not to have any complications of womankind till she was well acquainted and knew on whom she could count for help. She admitted to her own heart, too, that she could open up the plan to them, and teach a class in her own way, better stilling the flutter of her own frightened heart, if there were no women or girls about to watch.

She was disappointed, it is true, but after a moment she reflected that perhaps even Stephen's absence was an advantage. She would take this quiet hour to study up a lesson and plan her programme, though it would be much easier if she knew just what kind of scholars she was to have. She spent a happy morning and afternoon planning for the Sunday, and only toward night did she begin to feel uneasy and hover near the door looking down the road.

Marna came in, shaking her head and muttering again, and it required all Margaret's faith and bravery to keep her heart up.

The night closed down like that other night when she had kept a vigil, and still neither of the young men appeared. Margaret wished that Philip would come, so that she might reassure herself by asking where he supposed Stephen had gone and when he would return. She acknowledged to herself that after all there was something strong and good to lean upon in Philip.

She prayed much that evening, and by and by lay down and tried to sleep. After several hours of restless turnings she did finally fall into an uneasy sleep.

But, when the morning broke with its serene sunshine, and neither of the two men had returned, she grew more restless. In vain did she try to settle to anything. She constantly returned to look off down the road.

Marna said little that day; but Margaret remembered her former words, and her old anxieties returned to clutch her till she was driven to her knees. As she prayed, a great, deep love for her new-found brother grew and grew in her soul till she felt she *must* save him, for instinctively she knew that he needed saving more than many.

And the second day wore away into the night, but still they had not returned.

Margaret lived through various states of mind. Now she was alarmed, now indignant that they should treat her so; and now she blamed herself for having come out here at all. Then alarm would succeed all other feelings, and she would fly to her refuge and find strength.

When the third day dawned and seemed likely to be as the others had been, she questioned Marna as to where she thought they could have gone; but the old woman shut her lips and shook her head. She did not like to tell. She had watched the young girl long enough to have a tender feeling of protection toward her.

This third day was Saturday. Margaret had had some wild ideas of trying to saddle the horse and go out into the strange, unknown country to seek knowledge of her brother; but her good sense told her that this would be useless. She must wait a little longer. Some news would surely come soon. Resolutely she sat down to study the Sunday-school lesson just as if nothing had happened to disturb her, and to plan out everything for the morrow, trying to think that her brother would surely return for Sunday; but her heart sank low in trouble as the night came on once more, and she left her supper, which Marna had carefully prepared, untasted on the table while she stood by the dark window looking down the road.

Philip's anger had carried him far toward his destination. When at last it cooled with his bodily fatigue, and he began to reflect on the possibilities of what might happen during his absence, he would have been minded to turn back, but that his horse was weary and the day was far spent. Besides, it would be foolish to go back now when he had almost accomplished that for which he came. A few minutes with the man he sought would be all he needed, and perhaps he could exchange horses, or give his own a few hours' rest and then return. He hurried on, annoyed that it was growing so late.

There was some difficulty in finding the place, after all, for several old landmarks had been removed by a fire, and it was quite dark before he reached the lonely ranch of the man with whom he had business.

He had not known his own strong desire to return until he discovered how he was to be hindered. He found that the man whom he sought had gone to another ranch a few miles further on, and would probably not return for three or four days. It would be ridiculous to turn back and have his long journey for nothing. He must press on now and accomplish what he had come for. He got a fresh horse, and, taking only a hasty supper, spurred his horse forward through the darkness, trusting recklessly to his own knowledge of the country to bring him to the desired point.

Of course he lost his way, and brought up at the place the next morning when the sun was two hours high, only to find that the man whom he had come in search of had started back the afternoon before, and must be at home by this time.

Another delay, and another fresh horse, and he was on his way back, too weary to realize how long a strain he had been under. And, when he reached the first ranch and found his man, he was so worn out that he dared not start home without a few hours' sleep. So, the business disposed of, he lay down to sleep, his mind tormented the while by thoughts of Stephen and his own discarded trust.

But worn nature will take her revenge, and Philip did not awake until almost sunset on the second day. Then his senses came back sharply with a vision of Margaret, a dream perhaps, or only his first waking fancies. She seemed to be crying out in distress and calling: "My brother! Stephen! O, save him, Philip!" And with the sound of that dream voice there came a great desire in his heart to hear her speak his name that way.

But he put this from him. He tried to remember that he had been angry with her, and that this whole thing was her fault anyway for not following his advice, and then he remembered that she had no knowledge or reason to follow his advice—a stranger. What did she know of him and his reasons for what he had said? In some way she must be told, but how could he tell her?

All these thoughts were rushing through his mind as he went out and was hunting up his own horse, hastily preparing to go home. He would not have stopped for something to eat even, had his host not insisted. Then it was only because the reasonableness of this act appealed to him that he finally yielded and ate what he was given.

And all the long miles back, most of it in darkness, Philip was thinking, thinking, cursing himself for a fool that he had left Stephen alone with his sister, almost cursing God that such a state of things was possible.

It was toward morning when he neared the

handful of buildings that constituted the village near their home. The horse quickened his pace, and familiar things seemed to urge the travellers forward. Distant discordant sounds were in the air. A pistol-shot rang out now and again. But that was not unusual. Shots were as common as oaths in that neighborhood. They were a nightly occurrence, a part of a gentleman's outfit, like his generosity and his pipe. Nearer the sounds resolved themselves into human voices, the deep bark of dogs, singing, the clinking of glasses, a slamming shutter, the gallop of a rider whirling home after a night of revelry, to strike terror to the heart of any who waited for him.

The muscles around Philip's heart tightened as a sickening thought came to him, and he put spurs to his willing beast, making the road disappear rapidly behind him.

Near the one open house in the village, where lights were still burning and whence the sounds came, he drew rein, and the patient horse obeyed, having felt that anxious check to his rein before. Close under the window he stopped. Listening and then rising in his saddle, he looked to make sure of what his heavy heart had already told him was true.

There in the midst of the room, on a table,

his golden curls all disheveled, his jaunty attire awry, his fine blue eyes mad with a joyless mirth, and his whole face idiotic with absence of the soul that lived there, stood Stephen. He had evidently been entertaining the company, and he was speaking as Philip looked.

"Jes' one more song, boys!" he drawled. "I got a go home to my sister. Poor little girl's all alone, all aloney. Zay, boys, now that's too bad, ain't it?" His voice trailed off into unintelligibility.

A great anger, horror, and pity rose within Philip. Pity for the sister, anger and horror over her brother. He had seen Stephen like this before, and had sadly taken him away and brought him to himself, excusing him in his heart; but he had never before felt more than a passing disgust over the weakness of the man who put himself into such a condition. He had gone on the principle that, if Stephen liked that sort of thing from life, why, of course he had a right to take it; but he had always tried to save him from himself. Now, however, the thought of the sweet, trusting girl alone in the night waiting for him—how long had she waited?—while the brother she had come to help and love bandied her name and her pity around among a set of drunken loafers—

Philip stopped his thoughts short, and sprang into action.

Not in the quiet, careless way in which he usually entered upon such scenes and took possession of his partner did he come this time. His soul was roused as great men's are when they have a deed of valor to perform.

He strode into that maudlin company, and dashed men right and left. They rose from the floor in resentment, or reeled against the wall, and shook trembling fists, and felt for ready weapons; but Philip's wrath was mighty. They quailed before him. One word he uttered between set teeth and white lips.

"Fiends!"

Then he grasped the shrinking Stephen firmly, and dragged him from the table and from the room before the fiery men around him had realized and drawn their revolvers. One or two wild shots whistled harmlessly into the air after him, but he and Stephen were gone.

He put Stephen—already in a senseless state—upon his horse, and took him to a shanty where he knew that no one was living now; and all the rest of that night and through the brightness of Saturday he stayed guard over him.

Stern lessons of life he read to himself as he sat there watching the tainted beauty of the face lying before him. All Stephen's gay, winning qualities were hidden behind the awfulness of what the man had become. He had never seen it so before. He had simply borne with Stephen till he came out of one of these states and became his gay, companionable self again. Now all at once Philip looked with disgust upon him. And the difference was that up on the hill five miles away there sat a sweet, pure woman, whose trust and freely lavished love the man before him had basely betrayed.

When Stephen had slept long, Philip brought water, bathed his face, and made him drink. He was determined to make Stephen perfectly sober, and he was anxious to do this as soon as possible, that they might get home and relieve the anxieties of the girl who waited there. But it was a stern face that Stephen looked into from time to time, and it was a silent journey that they took that night when darkness had come down to cover them. Only one sentence Philip spoke as they neared the house, and it was in a tone that Stephen was not likely to disregard.

"Be careful what you say to your sister!"

Then Stephen wondered what had happened since he left home, and how many days he had been away, and sat soberly trying to think as he rode up to the house.

Margaret's white face met them at the door, and Philip spoke first, his tone anxious and earnest.

"I am afraid you have been lonely, Miss Halstead. I am sorry it happened so. You see, Stephen thought he must come after me, and we were delayed by the absence of the man we went to see. The ride was too much for Stephen. He is played out, I am afraid. He ought to go right to sleep. If you have any coffee there, I will carry him in a cup. It will do him good. No, he isn't sick, just used up, you know. Nothing to worry about."

Philip's voice was quite cheerful. If Margaret could have seen his face, she would have wondered at his tone. But Margaret had been sitting in the dark, and it took some minutes to light the lamp with her trembling fingers, shaking now from the relaxation of the strain.

"Hope I didn't scare you, Margaret," Stephen spoke, his gay, easy manner settling upon him like an old coat he had plucked from its familiar nail and fitted on. "You know one must not wait where duty calls. But I'll take Phil's advice, I guess, and turn in. I feel mighty seedy. All knocked up with the long ride."

Philip was soon back from caring for the horses, and took the smoking coffee from Margaret's hand. As she handed it to him, she looked into his face.

"How about you, Mr. Earle? You look as if you needed the coffee more than Stephen," she said kindly.

The tender tone was almost too much for Philip after the grim strain he had passed through. It had in it a note of his mother's voice when he used to come home with a bruise from a fall or a fight. He smiled faintly, and said most earnestly,

"Thank you!"

And when he came out from Stephen's room he found that she had set him a tempting supper on one end of the table.

She hovered about, waiting upon him till he was done, and told him to sleep late in the morning when she said good-night. Then she went to her room, buried her face in the pillow, and cried. She did not know why she was crying. It was not from trouble. Perhaps it was relief. When she grew calm, she thanked God for saving her from some nameless trouble that she felt, but did not understand, and begged of Him again help for the morrow and the work she was going to try to do for Him.

## 10

## *Margaret Faces an Unexpectedly Difficult Task*

THE HEALING of sleep settled down upon the little household late that Saturday night, and lasted far into the morning.

When Margaret awoke, the sun shone broad across her floor, and a sense of relief shone into her heart. As she went about her preparations for the day, an awe settled down upon her in remembering what she was going to try to do for Christ. She dared not think of any words she would speak, and she had not yet made up her mind how she would set about it to introduce her plan to the expected guests. She shrank as she remembered Byron's bold, handsome eyes, and wondered whether he would be among those invited, or whether he was Philip's friend alone. She shut her own eyes, and prayed that she might put away such thoughts and think only of the message she had to bring.

The two young men literally did as she told them, and did not awake until almost noon. Margaret had kept their breakfast waiting until it was too late, and then she hastened the dinner preparations; and so the first meal they ate together was dinner.

After dinner Philip hastened to the neglected horses, and to see after some matters at the barn, and Stephen threw himself upon the couch. The day was chilly, and Marna had kindled a fire on the hearth. It crackled pleasantly, and Stephen was feeling the relief that comes after a throbbing headache has ceased. He took up a book from his sister's case, and began to read. He seemed to have forgotten all about his company, and Margaret thought perhaps he had not invited them after all, and it would be best not to speak about it. He was tired, and it would be much better for him.

There was immense relief to her in the thought that her task, which at times assumed proportions impossible, would be put off indefinitely. And yet there came a strange pang of disappointment, for her careful study of the lesson had revealed to her hidden blessed truths which the Spirit had made her long to impart to others. She wondered whether she could muster courage to suggest to Stephen that he and she, and perhaps Philip, too, if he liked, study the lesson together. She was sitting shyly by the piano, looking at her brother behind his book, and meditating whether she should ask him about it, when the door burst open most unceremoniously, and three young men stood upon the threshold.

To be sure, they knocked uproariously upon the opening door, and their greeting was loud and hilarious. Margaret arose, startled. But they stopped as suddenly as they had begun, and looked about upon the strange, changed place. This was a room with which they were unacquainted, many times as they had ascended the hill to make good cheer for Stephen. And the woman who stood silent by the piano was a lady, and was beautiful beyond any question.

It was as if they had come expecting summer weather, and were suddenly plunged into a magnificent snowbank. They stood embarrassed and for the moment silent, just as the other two strangers had stood, a little while before. All the effrontery of their brave, outlandish Western attire deserted them. The instinctive feeling of each man was self-defence, and involuntarily their hands sought the place which held the inevitable weapon. Not that they meant to draw it, only to feel the cold, keen protection of its steel assuring them.

They had been gentlemen born, these three, at least in appearance, but had long ago forgotten what that word meant. Perhaps it was the harder for them, therefore, to understand the beauty of purity and art, having once known it and wandered so far from its path, than if they had never seen it.

They were wordless for the moment, not knowing how to occupy the new position.

Stephen came airily forward. He was glad Philip was out of the way for the time. He hoped he would remain away until things were well going.

"Welcome!" he said with a wave around the place as if it were a palace and he the king. "My sister, Margaret Halstead, gentlemen. Margaret, this is Bowman, and Fletcher, and Banks."

Margaret bowed in a stately way she had, which made her seem much taller than she really was, and kept at a distance any man whom she chose to keep so. Nevertheless, there was in her manner a smile of welcome, which seemed to the three strangers something like a cold bit of sunshine that had fallen their way and charmed them, but did not belong to them.

They came in and sat down, trying to assume their natural voices and easy speeches; but a mist of convention was enveloping them round, which they could not drive away. All but Banks.

Banks was small, slight, hard of feature, with an unfeeling slit of a mouth and hateful, twinkly black eyes that were not large enough to see anything wonderful. He carried about him an ill-fitting self-complacency that belonged to a much larger man. His collegiate career had been cut short by his compulsory graduation to an inebriate asylum and later to the West.

Banks essayed a remark to Margaret which would have caused Philip to sling him out the door if he had been there. It was complimentary and coarse in the extreme. Fortunately Margaret did not understand it, and stood in dumb amazement at the shout of laughter that was raised. She was glad when the door was darkened again by other guests, for she felt there was something painful in the atmosphere. She looked for Stephen to stand beside her; but he was already slapping shoulders with a newcomer, and her gaze met Byron's bold eyes bent in admiration as he came forward and attempted to take her hand by way of greeting, having a desire to show to the others his superior acquaintance with the queen of the occasion. But Margaret drew her hand behind her, and held him back with the gentle dignity of her greeting. He felt that she had not forgotten their last meeting and the words she had spoken to him. Her glance reminded him reproachfully of it. He saw he must not expect to be her friend with that between them. The blood stole up his swarthy cheeks, and he stood back conquered, to see Bennett—whom he knew to be no better than himself, but whom she did not know— greeted with a welcoming smile.

Bennett's white eyelashes fell beneath the glory of that smile, and his freckles were submerged in red. He sat down hard in a Morris chair that was several inches lower than he had expected, while Banks carolled out a silly song appropriate to the moment. This happened to be Banks's role, the bringing in of appropriate songs and sayings at the wrong minute, and causing a laugh.

Margaret looked about the room bewildered. The place seemed to be swarming with great, bold, loud, men. She remembered Philip's warning, and gasped. One moment more, and she felt that her head would be whirling dizzily. She must get command of the situation or fail. Surely her Strength would not desert her now, even though she had made a mistake. She lifted her soul to God, and wished while she prayed that Philip would come in. Philip somehow seemed so strong.

There were but seven men invited, though they looked so many. They were for the most part the pick of the country thereabout, at least among Stephen's friends. He had intended to be careful on Philip's account, for he knew Philip would not stand any one that would be outrageous. But Stephen's discretion had forsaken him with the first taste of liquor that passed his lips, and two had crept into the band worse than all the rest. Well for Margaret that she was strong in her ignorance of this.

"Well," began Stephen, and Margaret saw that now was her opportunity if she would not let this strange gathering slip from her control.

"My brother asked you to come this afternoon because he thought you might enjoy some music and reading," she said in a clear voice that commanded instant silence, "and I shall be very glad if I can give you any pleasure."

Then she smiled upon them like an undesired benediction, and each man dropped his eyes to his feet, and then raised them, wondering why he had dropped them.

"Won't you all sit down and make yourselves comfortable?" she went on pleasantly. "We should like to have you feel at home."

"Be it ever so humble, there's no place like home," sung out Banks flippantly.

"Shut up, Banks!" said Bennett, turning redder, and glaring from under his white eyelashes at his neighbor.

"I want to get acquainted with my brother's friends, of course," went on Margaret, not heeding this accompaniment to her words. She had suddenly the feeling that she was holding a pack of hounds at bay, much as one feels when starting a mission school of wild street arabs. She must say the right thing at once and work quickly, or her cause would be lost.

"I don't know what kind of music you like best; so perhaps you will excuse me to-day if I play you my own favorites. I'm going to begin at once, please, so that we shall have plenty of time for them all, because by and by I want you all to sing."

They looked at her as they might have watched some new star in a theatre, wondering, awed for the minute by the strangeness, but not permanently. It takes a great deal to awe a Western cowboy.

Margaret turned with a sweep of her white draperies, and sat down at the piano. As she did so, she caught a glimpse of Philip standing in the doorway, his rugged face written over with disapproval and anxiety. It spurred her to do her best; and, laying her fingers upon the keys, she imparted her own spirit to them.

Some music lay upon the rack before her. It was not what she had intended to play first, but it would do as well as anything. She felt she must waste no more time in beginning, for Philip's face looked capable of almost any action if there was sufficient cause.

It was Handel's "Largo" that sounded forth through the room with swelling, tender strain. She felt that perhaps it was not the right thing with which to hypnotize her audience, but she put her soul into it. If it were possible for music to express sacred things and true, then her music should do so. But, had she known it, music of any kind was so rare a treat and so unique that she might have played even a common scale for a few moments and had her audience until the strangeness wore away.

She gave them no time, however, to grow restless; for she glided from one thing to another, now a great burst of triumph, and now a tender sympathetic melody, and all of them connected in her own mind with sweet days of worship in her childhood's church at home. Instrumental music might not convey anything of a Sabbath nature to these untamed men, but it certainly could be no worse than no attempt at it, and she was feeling her way.

Philip stood like a grim sentinel in the doorway. The company felt his shadow and resented it, but were engrossed with the music at first. Philip could not let himself enjoy it. He stood as it were above it, and let it break like waves about his feet. He felt that he must, or some wave might ingulf them all.

He watched their faces as a great watchdog might eye intruders, mistrusting, lowering, a growl already in his throat.

The wonder of the spell the girl had cast about them had not yet touched him. He was guarding her.

Suddenly she felt the pressure of emotion too strong for her. With a chord or two she dealt "one imperial thunderbolt that scalps your naked soul," as Emily Dickinson has put it, and stopped.

They caught their breath, and, coming out from under the charm, turned toward Philip to take their revenge for his attitude.

But Margaret was all alert now. She felt the disturbance in the air. She moved quickly.

"You must be thirsty," she said, unconsciously using a term that meant more to them than she dreamed. "I'm going to give you a cup of tea. Stephen, call Marna to bring the kettle, please; and Philip, will you pass the cups?"

There was a gentle deference in her tone as she addressed Philip, almost as if she would ask his pardon and acknowledge that he was right about what he had told her.

There was something more also, a pleading that he would stand by her and help her out of this scrape into which she had allowed herself to go.

The soul of Philip heard and responded, and his quiet acquiescence sustained her all through the afternoon. It was as if there were some unspoken understanding between them.

The men watched her curiously as she moved about the room, collecting strange, thin, little dishes, the like of which some of them had never seen, and others had almost forgotten. There was enough of the unexpected and interesting about it to keep them moderately subdued, though a muttered oath or coarsely turned expression passed about now and again, and Banks tried a joke about the tea which did not take very well.

Margaret, however, was happily ignorant of much of this, though she felt the general pulse of the gathering pretty accurately.

The tea came speedily, for Marna had obeyed orders implicitly, and had been hovering near the door with a curious, troubled expression and shaking head. With the tea were served delicious little cakes of sugary, airy substance, olives, salted almonds, and dainty sandwiches.

The whole menu was just what Margaret would have used at home with her own friends. She knew no other way. Extravagant and unusual? O, certainly, but she did not realize this, and the very strangeness of it all worked for her anew the charm she had broken when she ceased to play, and kept the wild, hilarious spirits she would tame quiet till she had the opportunity for which she had been praying.

They vanished, these delectable goodies, as dew before the sun. The capacity of the company seemed unlimited. The entire stock of sweet, dainty things from carefully packed tin boxes that Margaret had brought with her would scarcely have sufficed to satisfy such illimitable appetites.

"They eat like a Sunday-school picnic," thought Margaret to herself, laughing hysterically behind the screen as she waited a minute to catch her breath before going out to try her hand at the most daring move of all her programme.

Then she looked across to where Philip stood watching her with faithfulness written in every line of his face, and saw that he was eating nothing. She motioned him to her, and gave him with her own hands a cup of tea. It was well she gave it behind the screen; for, had the others seen it, a bitter rivalry would have begun at once for favors from the lady's hand.

He took it from her as one might take an unexpected blessing, and drank it almost reverently, if such a thing can be.

Then he looked up to thank her; but she was gone, and he saw her standing, palm-surrounded, near the piano again, her soft white draperies setting her apart from the whole room, and her golden hair making a halo about her head, the rays of the setting sun just touched her with its burnished blessing, like a benediction upon her work. Philip felt, as he looked, that she was surrounded by some angelic guard and needed no help from him. His stern expression relaxed, and in its place came one of amazement.

She was talking now in low, pleasant tones, as if these men were all her personal friends. Each man felt honored separately, and dropped his gaze, that the others might not know.

She was telling them in a few words about her home, and how she had come out there alone to her brother, now that she was alone in the world. She was putting herself at their mercy, but she was also putting them upon their honor as men, if they had any such thing as honor. Philip was doubtful about that, but he listened and wondered more.

Then she told them about the first Sabbath she had spent here, and how shocked and disappointed she had been to find no church or Sabbath services going on near by. She told them how she missed this, till they could not but believe in her sincerity, though such a state of mind was beyond their ken entirely; and she spoke of her Sabbath-school class at home, and how she loved the hour spent with them, until each man wished he might be a little boy for the time being, and offer her a class.

"I haven't asked my brother if I may," she

said with a girlish smile, turning toward Stephen as he sat disturbed and uncomfortable in the corner. She felt intuitively that Stephen would count it a disgrace to be implicated in this matter, and she thus honorably exonerated him. "But I am going to ask whether you would not be willing to help me make up for this loss I have felt. Perhaps some of the rest of you have felt it too."

Here she gave a quick, searching look about the circle of sunburnt faces.

"I wonder if you will help."

They straightened up, one or two, and looked as if they would like to assent, but Margaret went quickly on. She did not want to be interrupted now till she was done; else she might not have courage to finish.

"I am going to ask if you will help me have a Sunday school, or Bible service, or something of that sort. I will try to be the teacher unless you know of some one better—"

There was a low growl of dissent at the idea that any one could equal her, and Margaret flushed a little, knowing it was meant for her encouragement.

"We could not do much as they do at home in the East, but it would be keeping the Sabbath a little bit, and I think it would help us all to be better. Don't you?"

She raised her eyes, at last submitting the question to them, and the slow blood mounted in each face before her, while shame crept up and grinned over each shoulder. When had any one ever supposed that they wanted to be helped to be better?

"Now, will you help me?" She asked it in a sweet, pleading voice, and then sat down to wait their decision.

## Margaret Makes the
## Great Endeavor

BUT shame does not sit easily upon such as Banks. He roused himself to shake it off. He seldom failed in an attempt of that sort. He saw his opportunity in the intense silence that filled the room.

> "I am a little Sunday-school scholar, lah,
>   lah,
> I dearly love my pa and ma, ma, ma, ma;
> I dearly love my teacher, too, too, too, too,
> And do whatever she tells me to—to, to, to,
> Teacher, teacher, why am I so happy,
>   happy—"

He had chanted the words rapidly in his most irresistible tone, and he expected to convulse the audience and turn the whole gathering into a farce; but he had sung only so far when strong hands pinioned him from behind, gagged him with a handkerchief, and would have swiftly removed him from the place but that Margaret's voice broke the stillness that succeeded the song. Her face was white, for she realized that she had been made the subject of ridicule; but her voice was sweet and earnest.

"O, not that, please, Philip. Let him go," she said. "I'm sure he will not do it again, and I don't think he quite understood. I don't want to urge anything you would not all like, of course. I want it very much myself, though, and I thought perhaps you would enjoy it too. It seems so lonely out here to me, without any church."

She sat down, unable to say more. It must be left with God now, for she had done all she could.

Then up rose bold Byron. It was his opportunity to redeem himself. "My lady," he began gallantly, "I ain't much on Sunday schools myself, never having worked along that line; but I think I can speak for the crowd if I say that this whole shootin'-match is at your disposal to do with as you choose. If Sunday school's your game, we'll play at it. I can sit up and hold a book myself, and I'll agree to see that the rest do the same if that'll do you any good. As for any better teacher, I'm sure the fellows'll all agree there's not to be found one within six hundred miles could hold a candle to you, so far as looks goes; and as for the rest we can stand 'most anything if *you* give it to us."

It was a long speech for Byron, and he nearly came to grief three times in the course of it because of some familiar oath that he felt the need of to strengthen his words.

Philip, as he held the struggling, spluttering Banks, glared at Byron threateningly during it all, and wondered whether he would have to gag the entire crowd before he was through; but Byron stumbled into his chair at last, and Margaret, to cover her blushes and her desire to laugh and cry both, put her hands up to her hot cheeks, and wondered what would come next. Then a wild, hilarious cheer of assent broke from the throats of the five other guests, and Margaret knew she had won her chance to try.

"O, thank you!" was all she could gather voice to say; but she put much meaning into her words, and the men felt that they had done a good and virtuous thing.

"Then we will begin at once," said Margaret, almost choking over the thought that she was really going to try to teach those rough big fellows a Bible lesson. "Mr. Byron, will you pass that pile of singing-books? and let us sing 'Nearer, my God, to Thee.' You must all have heard that, and I'm sure you can sing. Philip, please give this book to your friend, and release him so he can help us sing," and she actually was brave enough to smile condescendingly into Banks's mean little eyes.

Philip took the book, and let Banks go as he might have given a kick and a bone to a vagrant dog; but he looked at this most remarkable Sunday-school superintendent with eyes of wonder.

And they could sing, O, yes, they could sing! From their great throats poured forth a volume of song that would have shamed many an Eastern church choir. They sang as they would have herded cattle or forded a stream, from the glad, adventurous joy of the action itself; and more; they sang because they were trying to help out a lonely, pretty girl, who for some mysterious reason was to be helped by this most pleasant task.

As she played and listened to the words rolled forth, Margaret found in her heart a flood of uncontrollable desire that they all might know the meaning of those words, and sing them in very earnest.

The lesson, the same one that she would have taught, had she been at home with her class of little boys, began with the grand and thrilling statement:

"There is therefore now no condemnation to them that are in Christ Jesus, who walk not after the flesh, but after the Spirit."

They listened respectfully while she read the lesson in her clear voice. But the words conveyed very little to their minds, and it is doubtful, when she began to talk about a prisoner condemned to death and a pardon coming just in time to save him, whether they connected it in the least with the words she had been reading, or whether they even recognized them as the same she had read, when she repeated them later after having made the meaning clear.

It was simple language she used, with plain, everyday stories for illustrations; for she was accustomed to teaching little boys. But a doctor of theology could not have more plainly told the great doctrines of sin and atonement than did she to those men whose lives were steeped in sin, and to whom the thought of conviction of sin, or of condemnation, seldom if ever came.

They felt as if they had suddenly dropped into a new world as they listened, and some of them fidgeted, and some of them wondered, but all were attentive.

She did not make her lesson too long. For one thing, her own trembling heart would have prevented that. She had feared that she would not have enough to say to make the lesson of respectable length; but, when she began, the need of the souls before her appealed to her so strongly that she found words to bring the truths before them.

Philip watched her in amazement. She reminded him of a priestess robed in white, the palms behind her and her gold hair crowning her. He could think of nothing but Hypatia and her wonderful school of philosophy of old, as she opened up the simple truths. Looking about on the hard faces, softened now by something new and strange that had come over their feelings, he felt her power, and knew her way had been right; yet he feared for her, was jealous for her, hated all who dared to raise their eyes to hers.

What power was it that made her able thus to hold them? Was it the mere power of her pure womanhood? Or the fascination of her delicate beauty? No, for that would have affected such men as these in another way. They would have admired, and openly; but they would not have been quiet or respectful.

Another thought kept forcing itself to his mind. If the God whom she was preaching, whom she claimed as her Father, should prove indeed to be the one true God, was he, Philip Earle, condemned? But this thought Philip put haughtily aside.

"I have been thinking," said the teacher, "as I sat here talking, how beautiful it would be if Jesus Christ were yet on the earth so that we could see Him. What if He should walk into that door just now?" and she pointed to the doorway where they had all entered.

Involuntarily each man lifted his eyes to the door, and Philip with the rest.

"He would come in here, just as He used to come into households in those Bible times, and we would make room for Him, and you would all be introduced."

Some of the men moved restless feet. Their thoughts were growing oppressive.

"And you would all see just what kind of a man, and a Christ, Jesus is," went on the sweet voice. "You could not help admiring Him, you know. You would see at once how gracious He is. You would not be—I hope—I think—none of you would be like those people who wanted to crucify Him—though we do crucify Him sometimes in our lives, it is true; but if we could see Him and know Him it surely would be different. He would call you to be His disciples, just as He called those other disciples of His, Philip and Andrew and Matthew and John and Peter and the rest."

Unconsciously Philip Earle flushed and started at his name. She had never called him Philip until that afternoon, and he thought for the moment she was speaking to him now.

There were others who looked conscious, too, for Bennett's name was Peter, and Fletcher's name was Andrew, and two others bore the name of John. Because of these little coincidences they were the more impressed by what she said.

"And what would you answer Him?" She paused, and there was stillness for just a minute in the room.

"I am going to tell you what I want for you all." She said it confidingly. "It is that you shall know Jesus Christ, for to know Him is to love Him and serve Him. And suppose as we study in this class that you try to think of yourselves as men like those disciples of old, whom He has called, and that you are getting acquainted with Him and finding out whether you want to answer His call. Because until you know Him you cannot judge whether you would care enough for Him for that. Will you try to carry out my fancy?"

She had struggled much with herself to know what she should do about prayer. It did not seem right to have a service without it, and she did not feel that she could pray. It was unlikely that the others would be willing to do so. She had settled on asking them all to join in the Lord's Prayer until she saw them, and then she knew that would not do. She even doubted whether many of them knew it. Her faint heart had decided to go without prayer, but now in the exultation of the moment she followed the longing of her heart to speak to her Father.

"Please, let us all bow our heads for just a minute and keep quiet before God," she said, and the silence of that minute, wherein seconds were counted out by great heart-beats, was one whose memory did not fade from the minds of the men present through long years of after experiences.

Awful stillness, painful stillness! Banks could not bear it. All his weak flippancy seemed singled out and held in judgment by it. He wanted to escape, wanted to break forth in something ridiculous, and yet he was held silent by some Unseen Power, while the terrible seconds rolled majestically and slowly around him.

"O Jesus, let us all feel Thy presence here. Amen!" said Margaret as if she were talking to a friend.

Then she turned quickly to the piano, and before the raising of the embarrassed eyes that dared not look their comrades in the face, lest they should be discovered as having been bowed in prayer, soft chords filled the room, and Margaret's sweet voice rang out in song.

"Abide with me," she sang; "fast falls the eventide."

The room had grown quite dusky, lighted only by the glowing fire in the fireplace, which Philip had quietly replenished from time to time with pine-knots that sent fitful glares upon the touched and softened faces of the men, while they sat rapt in attention to the music.

A few more chords, and the melody changed,

> *"Weary of earth, and laden with my sin,*
> *I look at heaven and long to enter in;*

*But there no evil thing may find a home,*
*And yet I hear a voice that bids me, 'Come.'*

*"So vile I am, how dare I hope to stand*
*In the pure glory of that holy land?*
*Before the whiteness of that throne appear?*
*Yet there are hands stretched out to draw*
*    me near."*

Soft chords came in here, like angel music that seemed to float from above them somewhere. It was a way she had with the piano, making it speak from different parts of the room and say the things she was feeling. The listeners half looked up as if they felt there were white hands stretched toward them.

The sweet voice went on:

*"It is the voice of Jesus that I hear,*
*His are the hands stretched out to draw me*
*    near,*
*And His the blood that can for all atone,*
*And set me faultless there before the throne.*

*"O Jesus Christ, the righteous! live in me,*
*That, when in glory I Thy face shall see,*
*Within the Father's house my glorious dress*
*May be the garment of Thy righteousness.*

> *"Then Thou wilt welcome me, O righteous*
> *Lord;*
> *Thine all the merit, mine the great reward;*
> *Mine the life won, and Thine the life laid*
> *down,*
> *Thine the thorn-plaited, mine the righteous,*
> *crown."*

"And now will you all sing a few minutes?" said their leader, turning toward them in the firelight, her fair face filled with the feeling of the prayer with which her song had closed.

"Philip, will you give us some light? Now let us sing 'I need Thee every hour' before you go home."

They growled out all their superfluous, bottled-up feelings into that song, and made it ring out, till Marna crept around and peered into the window to watch the strange sight. She stood there muttering in amaze, for such a miracle she never saw before. Perhaps Missie could work charms on even her, if she could make those wild fellows sit quiet there and sing that way.

And then they found themselves dismissed.

"I shall expect you next Sunday at the same time," she said, smiling, "and thank you so much for helping. It has been so good, almost like a Sunday at home. I have a delightful story and a new song for you next Sunday."

Greater marvel than all the rest, they went out quietly beneath the stars, mounting their horses in silence, and rode away. One attempt on Banks's part came to a dismal failure. Philip, standing at the door, heard the silly, swaggering voice rollicking through the night,

*"I dearly love my teacher, too, too, too, too,"*

and Bennett's unmistakable roar, "Shut up, you fool, can't you?" as the song was brought to a summary close.

Byron had dared to linger a moment by the teacher's side, and with an expression almost earnest on his face had asked,

"Aren't you ever going to forgive me?"

"You must go to the One you insulted for forgiveness," answered Margaret gravely. "When you have made it right with Him, I will be your friend."

Then Byron dropped his boastful head, and walked away silent and thoughtful.

They turned, then, Philip and Margaret, and found themselves alone. They could hear Stephen slamming around in his room, the thud of first one boot and then the other thrown noisily across the floor. Stephen evidently was not in a good humor.

Margaret's face grew sad, and she realized that through the whole afternoon her thoughts had been more taken up with the others than with the brother she had come to try to save. Had the message reached him at all?

Seeing Philip standing in the door watching her, the look of wonder still upon his face, her expression changed. She went over to where he stood, and, putting out one hand, touched him gently on the coat-sleeve. "I did not understand," she said simply. "You were right. I ought to have listened to you."

He looked down at the little hand with finger-tips just touching the cuff of his sleeve, as if it had been some heavenly flower fallen upon him by mistake; and then he said, his voice all strange and shaking: "No, it was I who did not understand. You have been *wonderful!*"

12

## "I Will Try"

THE DAYS passed busily now. The queer little dwelling on the hill grew in beauty and interest with every passing hour. Stephen did his part, and seemed pleasant enough about it, although the first few days after the Sunday school he was strangely moody and quiet. Margaret could not tell whether or not he was pleased with what she had done.

And now she lured the two young men to gather around the hearth in the evenings while she read aloud to them in carefully selected books which touched their experiences of life and made them forget themselves for a little while. Margaret's power of song was equalled only by her ability to read well; and no dialect, be it negro or Scotch, was too difficult for her to enter into its spirit and interpret it to her readers. So long had they been out of the world that some of the best books about which people had raved for a few days and then forgotten had passed them by entirely. These were among her favorites, and now she brought them out and read them, while the two sat by and listened, much moved, but saying nothing except to laugh appreciatively at some fine bit of humor.

Thus she read "Beside the Bonnie Brier Bush," "A Singular Life," "Black Rock," and "The Sky Pilot"; and then went further back to George Macdonald, and chose some of his beautiful Scotch stories, "Malcolm," "The Marquis of Lossie," and "Snow and Heather." Over this last they were as silent as with the rest, but now and then Margaret noticed that Stephen covered his face with his hand and Philip turned his eyes away from the light while she was reading about the "Bonnie Man."

This sort of thing was all new to the two lonely fellows, who were used to making companions of the woods and fields and dumb beasts, and letting life go for little. This world of the imagination peopled life more richly. But ever when a book was finished Stephen would grow restless, and sometimes go off upon his horse, and Philip too would disappear. When they returned,—it might be late the same night, or after a day had passed,— Margaret could not tell which of the two, if either, had been the one who started first, and her heart grew heavy.

She rode with Stephen or with both of them quite frequently now, and was getting to be an expert horsewoman. She knew the ways about the country, and had seen some beautiful views. But not once had either of her escorts taken her near to the railroad station where she had arrived, nor pointed out what she fancied must be the semblance of a village. When she asked them, they always put her off, and more and more she wondered why.

With some trepidation she faced the next Sabbath, half fearful that her class would come again, half fearful lest they should not. But they came, every one, and brought two or three others along. There was not much need for Philip to stand guard, as he did, at the rear of the company, ready to spring should any slightest insult be offered to the teacher.

They had odd ways, these rough scholars of hers, and were as undisciplined as a company of city ragamuffins; but they respected the beautiful girl who chose to amuse herself by amusing them, and they listened quietly enough.

After the first wonder wore away they had the air of humoring her whimsical wishes. It pleased them to take it this way. It helped them to humble themselves into respectful attention. But ever, now and again, some word of hers would strike home to their hearts; and there would come that restless, noisy moving of the feet, that dropping of the eyes and avoiding one another's gaze, as each tucked his own past away within his breast, and fancied no one knew.

They grew to love the singing, and put their whole souls into the hymns they sang together; but they liked it more when Margaret sang to them the songs which sometimes brought back to them the days when they had been innocent and pure.

There was always, too, that solemn hush, that moment of silent prayer, before the one trembling but trustful sentence Margaret spoke to God. And sometimes, as the weeks went by, this or that man would find himself saying over in his own heart that sentence she had prayed the week before. It was not often she used the same sentence. Always it was something that touched the heart-experience or impressed the lesson-thought upon the mind.

The first prayer she had uttered in that house would always remain with Philip—"O Jesus, let us all feel Thy presence here." And, as he looked about the glorified room, it did seem as if a Presence had entered there, and come to stay. He often thought, as he sat waiting for the reading to begin in the evenings, of how that room had looked the night her letter came, and of how much he had hated the thought of her coming. Now, how light would go out of his life, should she go away! She did not know that. She never would, most likely. She was as far above him as the angels of heaven, but her coming had been as a gift from heaven. Would it last? Would she care to stay and keep it up? And Stephen, sitting on the other side of the hearth! Who could tell what were his thoughts as he alternated between his fits of moody silence and gay restlessness?

There came a day when Philip and Stephen were at work upon some fences, mending weak places where the cattle had broken them down. And in the afternoon Margaret put on a thin white dress with a scarlet jacket, and wandered out to where they were at work.

The day was bright and warm for late October, really hot in the sun. The light scarlet jacket was almost superfluous, but it served to intensify the scarlet in the landscape; and so she came, a bright bit of color into the prosaic of their work.

She had meant to talk to Stephen. In her heart she had been keeping some precious words she meant to say to him as soon as an opportunity offered. She longed to see him give himself to Christ. As yet she saw no sign that he had even heard the call to become a disciple.

But Stephen was in his most silent mood. He answered her in monosyllables, and at last gathered up his tools and said he was going to the other end of the lot. She saw it would do no good to follow him, for he was not in a spirit to talk; so, saddened and baffled, she walked slowly along by the fence toward the house. Until she came close to where he stood she had not noticed that Philip was working now right in the way where she would have to walk.

He stood up, and welcomed her with a smile, and offered her a seat on a low part of the fence, where the rails had some of them been taken down.

It came to her that perhaps her message to-day was for Philip rather than Stephen; so she climbed up and sat down.

He stood leaning against the supporting stakes near her, and the breeze caught a fragment of her muslin gown, and blew it gently against his hand. It was a pleasant touch, and his heart thrilled with the joy of her presence so near him. The muslin ruffle reminded him, with its caressing touch, of the wisp of hair that had blown across his face in the dark the night she had come.

A great, overpowering desire to tell her that he loved her came to him, but he put it aside. She was as cool as a lily dropped here upon this wayside, and talked with him frankly. But there was a something in their intercourse this afternoon more like their first brief talk about the moon than there had been since the night she came. She seemed to understand what he was saying, and he to interpret her feeling of the things in nature all about them. He dropped his tools, and stood beside her, willing to enjoy this precious moment of her companionship.

She looked across the fields to the valley, the other hills beyond, and a purple mountain in the distance, while he followed her gaze.

"You see a picture in all that," he said briefly, as if reading out her thoughts.

She smiled.

"Was it for all this that you gave up your home and friends, and came out here to stay?"

His face darkened.

"No," he said, "I was a fool. I thought life's happiness was all in one bright jewel, and I had lost mine."

"O," she said, looking at him searchingly, sorrowfully. "And, when you found out that was not so, why did you not go back?"

"Perhaps I was a fool still." He spoke drearily. He would not tell her the reason why he had stayed.

There was silence for a few minutes while each looked at the dreamy mountains in their autumn haze, but neither noted much of what was to be seen.

"There is a jewel you might have, which could not be lost. It is a pearl. The pearl of great price. Do you know what I mean?"

"Yes, I understand," he answered, deeply moved, "but I am afraid that would be impossible."

"O, why?" said Margaret, with pain in her voice. "Don't you care the least in the world to have it? I thought I saw a look of longing in your face last Sunday when we talked about Jesus Christ. Was I mistaken?"

Then she had been watching him and cared. Last Sunday! The thought throbbed in his throat with a delirious joy. He lifted his hand, and laid it firmly on the bit of fluttering muslin on the rail beside him. It was all he dared do to show his joy that she cared even so much.

"No, you were not mistaken," he said, his voice choking with earnestness. "I would give all I own to feel as you do, but I cannot believe in your Jesus as more than a man of history. If it were true, and I could believe it, I would be His slave. I would go all around the world searching for Him till I found Him if He were upon earth. But I cannot believe. I would not shake your sweet belief. It is good to know you feel it. It makes your life a benediction to every one you meet. Don't let my scepticism trouble you, or make you doubt."

"O, it couldn't!" said Margaret quickly, decidedly. "You could not shake my belief in Jesus any more than you could shake my belief in my mother, or my father, you know. Because I have known them. If you should tell me I had not had a mother, and she was not really good and kind to me, I should just smile, and pity you because you had never known her. But *I have,* you know. I do not blame you, for you have never known Jesus. You have not felt His help, nor almost seen Him face to face. You don't know what it is to talk with Him, and know in your heart He answers, nor to be helped by Him in trouble. You think I imagine all this. I understand. But you see I KNOW that I do not imagine it, for *I* have *felt.* You may feel too, if you will."

"I wish I might," said Philip with a sigh.

"'And ye shall find me, when ye shall search for me with all your heart,'" quoted Margaret softly, wistfully. "And there is another promise for such as you. God knew you would feel so, and He prepared a way. 'He that doeth His will shall know of the doctrine, whether it be of God—'"

"Do you really think that is true?" asked Philip, looking into her eager face.

"I know it is. I've tried it myself," she replied with emphasis.

There was a silence broken only by the whisperings of some dying leaves among themselves.

"Won't you take that promise, and claim it, just as you would take a bank-bill that promised to pay so much money to you, and present it for payment? Won't you do it—Philip?"

She had never called him that before except the first day of the Sunday school. It seemed to have been done then as a half-apology to him for not following his advice. After that day she had gone back to the formal "Mr. Earle" when she was obliged to address him by name at all.

Philip started, and crushed the bit of muslin between his fingers. He was deeply affected.

"How could I?" he said softly. Margaret caught her breath. She felt the answer to her prayer coming.

"Just begin to search for Him with all your heart, as if you KNEW He was somewhere. You never have tried to find Him, have you?"

"No."

"Then try. Kneel down to-night, and tell Him just how you feel about it, just as you have told me. Talk to Him as if you could see Him. You may not feel Him right away; but by and by, when your whole heart is in it, you will begin to know. He will speak to you in some way, until you are quite sure. Take as many other ways to find out, too, as you can, all the ways there are, of course; not that it matters so much, though, about your mere reason's being convinced; for, when you have felt Him near, you will KNOW against any kind of reasoning. But take the way of talking with Him. It is the quickest way to find Him."

"But should I not feel like a hypocrite, talking to One in whom I do not believe, of whose existence I have even no assurance?"

"No, for you said you wanted to find Him. It would be reaching out for what your heart desires, just as the untaught heathen do."

Philip flushed.

"You think I am a heathen," he said reproachfully.

"No, Philip, only a child of God, lost in the dark. I want you to find the way back."

"But suppose I do this, and nothing comes of it. Then you will be disappointed."

"What has that to do with it?" she said with a motion as of putting any thought of herself aside; "and something *will* come of it. No soul ever went to God in that way and nothing came of it. Besides, there is more you can do. There is the other promise, 'He that doeth His will.' After you have come to Him, and told Him that you want to find Him, but you cannot believe, and have asked Him to show you how, you can set to work to *do* His will. For through the doing what He would like to have you do a part of Himself will be revealed. Now, will you go to Him and tell Him all about it, to-night, and begin to try to find Him? Will you?"

Philip had drawn his hat low over his eyes, and stood looking off to the crimsoning sky. The sun had sunk low as they talked, and the air was growing chill. Margaret, in her intentness, did not know how grateful she was for the warmth of the little scarlet jacket. She waited silently and prayed while Philip thought.

At last he turned to her, and held out his hand with a grave smile.

"I will try," he said.

"With all your heart?" asked Margaret, as she laid her little white hand in his.

"With all my heart," he said reverently, as he looked into her eyes and pressed the hand he held.

Margaret let him know by the quick pressure of her hand-clasp how glad she was.

"And I shall be praying, too," she said softly.

Philip's heart quickened. It seemed to him like a holy tryst.

The young man picked up the idle tools, and they started toward the house, walking slowly through the twilight. They did not say much more. They were thinking of what had been said and promised. It was enough to walk quietly together thus and know what had passed. Stephen was not in sight. He must have gone to the house some time before.

But, when they came in and were ready to sit down to supper, he had not come yet, and Philip went out to call him.

Margaret listened to his shouts, strong, deep, full, with a note of earnest purpose in them. They grew more distant, and she thought he must have gone back to the lot where they were that afternoon to see what was keeping Stephen. She waited a long time by the door, and they did not come, and then she went in to search out the book she wanted to read to them that evening. Marna was keeping supper hot in the kitchen.

Suddenly there came a sound of rapid horse-hoofs down the road. She rushed to the door, and looked out. Down against the western sky, which still kept a faint blush from the sunset, now gone on its way to conquer other days, she saw a rider, hatless, galloping, etched for a moment against the sky. Then he was gone.

A sudden fear filled her heart. She put her hand to her throat, and rushed to the kitchen.

"Marna," she cried insistently, "did my brother come to the house before we did?"

The old woman shook her head.

"Brother rode off fast 'fore dark," she said doggedly, as if she did not wish to tell, but had to.

"Marna," said the girl, catching the old woman's arm in a grasp that must have been painful, "you talked about brothers drinking. I want you to tell me true if you know anything about it. Does my brother go where they drink?"

The old woman shut her lips, and a stubborn look came into her eye. She did not reply.

"Quick! Tell me at once," said Margaret, stamping her foot in her excitement. "Do they both drink? Is that why Stephen and Philip go away so suddenly sometimes? Do they both drink?"

"No!" said the old woman quickly. "Not both drink. One all right. Pretty good man. He take care. Bring other home. Heap good man."

"Which one, Marna?"

"Big man, heap good," answered Marna.

"And my brother drinks?" demanded Margaret, the sad truth hers now. "Answer me."

The old woman hung her head and nodded. It was as if she felt responsible.

Margaret had let fall the arm she held so tight, and was standing still for one brief minute with her hand upon her heart, too frightened to cry out, too bewildered even to frame a prayer; but her heart was waiting before God to know what she should do. Then swift as thought she turned, and, snatching up her little scarlet jacket as she ran, fled toward the barn.

The old woman looked up to try to say something comforting, and saw her vanish through the open door. She hobbled after her, some faint idea of protection coming to her withered senses. She found her in the barn with white, set face, struggling with the buckles of the saddle-girth. The two empty stalls beside the one remaining horse had made good her fears.

It was the poor old horse that had been left, for Philip needed the best in his chase through the night. Margaret had never ridden this horse, but she did not stop to think of that.

"Buckle this!" she commanded, as Marna came wondering into the barn, and she held the lantern that Philip had left lighted to find his own saddle.

"Missie no go out 'lone," pleaded Marna after she had done the bidding of the stern little voice. "Missie get lost. Big man find brother. Bring home. Missie stay with Marna."

"I must go," said Margaret quietly in tones of awful purpose. She swung herself into the saddle without stopping to think, as she usually did, how she was ever to get up to that great height. And she was doing it alone now.

"Now hand me the lantern!" she commanded, and Marna obeyed, her hand trembling. Tears from the long-dried fountains of her soul were running down her cheeks.

The old horse seemed to catch her spirit, and started off snorting as if he felt battle in the air. Some instinct carried him after the others who had sped along that road but a few minutes before. Or perhaps he had been that way before so many times that he could think of only one direction to take as he flew along.

Margaret held her seat firmly, grasping the lantern and the bridle with one hand, and tried to think and pray as the night wind, wondering, peered into her face, then turned and gently crept with her, protectingly, as if it thought she needed guarding.

13

## A Ride for Life

MARGARET had forgotten all her fears of former rides, lest the horse should stumble or take fright, lest the saddle should slip or she be thrown. Even the dark had lost its terror.

Somewhere near here the road cut away sharply at its outer edge, and went down to a great depth. She might be even now close upon it, and any moment the horse's feet slip over the precipice. But her heart trembled not. The Father was watching. She must go to find her brother.

Just why it was strongly borne in upon her that she must go herself, and not wait for Philip to find Stephen, perhaps Margaret could not have told. It may have been a wish to see for herself just what was Stephen's danger. Possibly, too, it was fear for Philip. Were

Marna's words true? "The big man no drink."
O, what comfort if she might be sure of that!
What a tower of strength would Philip then
become!

Riding, and praying, and trusting to God,
she was carried safely through the dangers of
a short cut that Philip, knowing and fearing,
had avoided, and she galloped into the main
road only a moment after Philip had passed
the spot.

The moon stood out like a silver thread
hung low and useless against the horizon. It
made but little difference in the darkness.

Margaret felt anxious to catch up with Philip
if possible, or at least get within sight of him. It
would not do to catch him too soon, or he
would send her back; and that she could not
bear. So she pushed on, and after a short time
could hear the sound of his horse and catch
fitful glimpses of a dark form riding hard.

By and by she came out upon a bridge
across a gully deep as darkness; how deep she
could not see as she peered down for one
awful glimpse, and then closed her eyes, and
dared not look again. It was too late to turn
back, for the way was scarcely wide enough
for that, and the bridge swayed horribly with
the horse upon it.

She held her breath as if that would make her weight the lighter, and dared not think until she felt the horse's feet touch solid ground. Then behind her came a snap, as sharp as if some giant tree had parted, and something, a bit of timber from the rail, perhaps, fell far and long below.

If the bridge had been one foot longer, or the horse had been going a little slower, horse and rider might have been lying down below in that sea of dark trees. The lantern slipped from her trembling hand, and fell crashing in the road; but the horse flew on, frightened, perhaps, by the danger he must have felt, following habit, too, in these long, wild rides to a certain goal he knew, and had travelled toward many a time before the new third horse came to be used in his stead.

But Philip had not crossed the crazy bridge that had been for some time now discarded, and indeed was supposed to be blocked by logs across its entrance. Either the old horse had jumped the logs in the dark, or some one had dragged them away to use somewhere else.

Philip, further down the road, had crossed by the new bridge, and had not known of the rider rushing along through dangers so profound.

He heard the crashing of the falling rail, and
the sound of flying hoofs a moment later. He
checked his horse, wondering who could be
riding behind him. For a moment the possibility that Stephen had not got ahead of him,
after all, but had tried to blind him by going
another way, passed through his mind; but he
looked back and saw only the darkness, and
heard the steady thud of the horse's feet. It was
not like the gait of Stephen's horse. He pushed
on; but occasionally he halted once more,
pursued by the feeling that he ought to wait
till that rider came up with him.

Then from out the darkness twinkled the
lights of the village below him. In a few
minutes he would be at his journey's end. He
could see the flare of the saloon lights now, and
almost hear the tinkle of the glasses and the
sliding of the wooden chairs upon the
wooden floor. He paused once more, for the
other horse was very near now. It would do no
harm to wait a second.

Then from out the night he heard his name
called once, in a wild, frightened cry, like a sob,
as of some one whose breath was almost gone,

"Philip!"

He stopped and waited as the horse came
swiftly toward him, something white taking

shape upon its back, till he saw the girl, her face white like her dress, her hair all loosened by her ride, unheld by any hat.

One word he spoke.

"Margaret!"

He had never used her name before in speaking to her. He did not know he used it now. But she did, even in her fright; and it seemed to give her courage and renewed strength.

"Don't stop; keep on!" she cried as her horse almost swept by him and he was forced to start his own horse again to keep alongside of her. "Don't lose a minute's time. I know all about it now. Let's hurry!"

"But, Margaret, you must not go!" he cried, putting out his hand to catch the bridle. "Why did you come? And how? It cannot be you crossed the broken bridge."

"It broke just after we got across, I think," she shuddered. "But do not think about it now. I am here. I cannot go back alone, and you must not turn back with me. Let us hurry on to save Stephen."

"But you cannot go down there. It is not safe for a woman."

"I am going, Philip. I am going to save my brother. And God is with us. There is no danger." In some way she managed to impart her eagerness to the old horse, and before Philip knew what she was doing she flew down the road far ahead of him.

It of course took but a moment for him to catch her again; but their gait was too rapid now to admit of talking, and the lights of the saloon were straight ahead. The horses knew their goal, and were making for it with all their might.

They stopped by the open window, from which coarse laughter was issuing into the night, foul with words and thick with oaths. Margaret raised her eyes, and saw what she had come to seek, her brother Stephen, standing gayly by the bar, a glass of something just raised to his smiling lips.

Stopping not to think of her unbound hair or the rough men staring all about, she slid from the horse, cast the bridle from her, and ran to the open door, from which a wide shaft of light was lying on the darkness of the pathway.

Like a heavenly Nemesis she appeared before their astonished gaze, and some who had already drunk deep that night thought she was the angel of the Lord sent to strike them dead.

She stood there in her limp white drapery, with long golden hair and outstretched arms, and only the vivid scarlet of the little jacket gleaming here and there like a flame among the glory of her hair.

She rushed to her brother, and dashed the glass from his hand even as he held it to his lips; then, turning to the roomful, she looked at them with one long, mournful, pitying, condemning glance. There were her Sabbath class to a man, standing before her. They were not drunk, for most of them could stand a good deal of liquor.

She said not one word to them, but just searched each face with a quick, heartrending glance, then turned, and drew her brother away.

Philip had tried to stop her as she flew from her horse to the open door; but she vanished from his hand like a thing of the air, and now he stood behind her ready to protect or help, even with his life. But she needed no help. Like darkness before the light they fell at her coming; and no one, not even Banks, raised a word or a laugh at her expense.

Even Stephen yielded unwillingly, and followed her from the room. Out into the night she led him, silently to Philip, with none to hinder or scoff. It was as if a messenger from God had walked into that saloon and plucked

Stephen away, searching each soul that stood there with one glance of flame.

The little cavalcade started out into the night; and as the sound of their going died away from the silent throng inside the lighted room, each man drew apart from the rest, moving noiselessly out into the darkness, and went his way by himself. The saloon was utterly deserted except by one or two old topers too sodden with drink to understand. The barkeeper cursed the girl who had thus descended and stopped business for that evening. But he soon put up his shutters and turned out his lights.

All silently the three rode, and the tired horses moved slowly. Stephen went ahead with bowed head, whether in anger or in shame they could not tell. Margaret and Philip rode abreast. Not a word they spoke as they went through the dark. Once Philip turned and looked at the frail girl by his side, her white face and gown lighting up the darkness. He thought she was shivering, and he silently took off his own coat, and buttoned it around her. She tried to protest by a lifted hand; but he would not be denied, and she smiled wanly, and let him fasten it around her. By common consent their communication was wordless. Stephen was close in front.

When they came out on the road near where Philip had first heard Margaret's call, he reached out, took her cold, white hand that lay limp on the saddlecloth, and held it in his warm, strong one all the rest of the ride. Again she let him have his way, and took comfort in the reassuring pressure.

When they reached home, she did not burst into tears and hang about Stephen's neck, begging, pleading, and reproaching. She was too wise for that, and her trouble much too deep.

She made him lie down on the couch by the fire. She brought some strong coffee that Marna had ready, and an inviting supper, and tried to make him eat. But, when she bent over him to ask whether he would sit up, she saw that upon his face there were tears that he had turned away to hide. Then she stooped and kissed him; and, kneeling there beside him with her face near to his, she prayed, "O Jesus Christ, save my dear brother!"

She kissed him again, and drew a little table close with the supper upon it, leaving him to eat it when he would, while she prepared something for herself and Philip.

Unreproached by any words, Stephen went to his room a little later and laid him down, more miserable than he had ever been in the whole of his gay, reckless life. Thoughts that till now had been too grave to be admitted to his mind entered and had their way. Searching questions he had never asked himself were poured upon him. Through them all he heard, and could not keep from hearing, his sister's voice on the other side of the thin board partition as she prayed and pleaded for her brother's salvation.

All night long he wrestled with the two spirits that were at war over him: the spirit of the demon that cried for drink, aroused by the few drops that had but wet his lips ere the glass was dashed from them; and the spirit of God's Holy One who strove to have him for eternity.

He sat dejectedly beside the fire the next morning after breakfast. His young face showed the wear of the night in haggard lines. He looked up as Margaret came over to him, and smiled wearily.

"I'm not worth it," he said. "You'd better give me up."

Margaret came and sat down beside him.

"I will never give you up, Stephen, until you are safe," she said.

He reached out and took her hand.

"You are a good sister," he said. That was all, but she felt that hereafter he would not be against any effort she made in his behalf.

It seemed as if he could not let her out of his sight the next few days; if she left the room, he followed her, and when he closed his eyes he saw a vision of his sister in white with burnished golden hair like some sweet angel of mercy come to save.

When the Sabbath came, Margaret doubted whether she would have any class but Stephen and Philip. Her heart was heavy over them all. More than she knew had she hoped that they were being led near to Christ. Now all her hopes were gone. Of what use was it to pray and preach and sing to men like this? Men who could stand about and watch quietly or help on the degradation of one of themselves. She had been reading deep lessons of the morals of that country ever since she came, but not until that night in the saloon had she realized how little she had to build upon with any of them. She even looked at Philip doubtfully sometimes. How could he be different from the rest, since he was one of them?

Philip had not presumed upon the intimacy of that night's wild ride. He was the same quiet, respectful gentleman, only with this difference: there was a promise between them; and, when he looked at her, his eyes always seemed to let her know he had not forgotten it.

But contrary to her expectations the entire company of men trooped in at the regular hour, and seated themselves, perhaps with a little more ostentation than usual.

Margaret welcomed them gravely. She was not sure of them, even though they had come. Marna had been telling her just before dinner about a circus, and a painted lady who was to dance in the saloon that afternoon.

"Men no come to-day," she had said. "If come, no stay late. Go see dance-woman."

Margaret's heart had sunk. Of what use was it for her to try to help these men if they were going straight to perdition as soon as she was through?

Margaret's fingers trembled as she played, and she had chosen minor melodies with dirge-like, wailing movements. The singing even was solemn and dragged, for the men only growled instead of letting out their usual voices.

They turned to the lesson, and Margaret read the text; but then she pushed the Bible from her and lifted troubled eyes to them, eyes in which tears were not a stranger. There was helpless despair in her attitude.

"You came here because I asked you to help me start a Sunday school, but I am afraid I have done you more harm than good," she said. The tragedy of it all was in her voice.

"You have been studying for a good many weeks now about Jesus Christ. I have told you how He loves you, and wants you, and how He took the trouble to leave his Home and come down here to suffer that you might be saved from sin, and come home to live with Him. It hasn't seemed to make a bit of difference. You have listened just to humor me, but you haven't done a thing to please Him, my dearest Friend, for whom I did it all. You have kept right on in your wrong ways. You have gone to places that you knew He would not like. You are planning, some of you, perhaps, to go to a wicked place this afternoon when we are through with the lesson. I have been showing you the right way, and you have chosen the wrong. It would be better for you that you did not know the right than, knowing it, that you should not take it. I have made a great mistake. I have shown you the loveliness of Christ, and you have treated it with indifference."

Her lips quivered, and she turned away to

hide the tears that came. The nights of anxiety and the days of excitement were telling on her nerves. She could not for the moment control her sadness. She put up both hands, and covered her face.

The silence was profound.

Then up rose Bennett in his might, he of the white eyelashes and the red hair. His face was mantled with blushes, but there was a true ring to his voice.

"My lady," he said,—it was the way they spoke of her with a deferential inflection that made it something different from the ordinary way of saying that,—"we're pretty rough, I know, and you can't say anything too bad about us, perhaps; but we ain't that bad that we're ungrateful, *I* know. We promised to stick by this thing, and we're a-going to do it. I don't know just what it is you want, and I don't think the other fellows sense it; but, if you just speak up, we're with you. If it's the drinking you mean, we'll shut up that saloon if you say so, though it'll be a dry spot fer some of us without it. And, if it's that there dancing-woman, if a single feller goes out of this room with intentions of visiting her scene of action, he goes with a bullet in him."

Bennett paused, and held his deadly weapon

gleaming before him, covering the whole room with it. Banks started back in terror, and then recovered himself and laughed nervously; but the other men faced Bennett steadily, and their silence lent consent. It was evidently understood so by Bennett, for he put the revolver back in his hip pocket, and resumed the unusual labor of his speech.

"As fer treating any One with indifference, we ain't meant to. It's just our way. We've listened respectful like to what you said about Him, and ain't questioned but what it's all so. But we ain't just up to this Sunday-school act, and don't know what to do. If you'd just say plain what 'tis you want, we might be able to please."

Margaret turned her eyes all bright with tears to the young man, and said with earnestness:

"I want you to be like Him, Mr. Bennett, to live like Him, to love Him, to grow to look like Him. That is what He wants. That is why He sent the message to you."

Bennett stood abashed at the awful disparity between the One spoken of and himself. He looked at her helplessly.

"I'll be gashed if I know what you mean,"

he replied with fervor; "but, if you'll make it all out easy fer us, we'll try."

It was late that night before she sent them away, for she had prolonged the lesson and the singing, and then had read them a tender story, full of the tragedy, the love, and the salvation of life.

They rolled forth their closing song with their magnificent voices as if they meant it. The words were,

> *"Just as I am, without one plea,*
> *But that Thy blood was shed for me,*
> *And that Thou bidd'st me come to Thee,*
> *O Lamb of God, I come, I come."*

They were all there yet. Not one of them had stolen away to the revelries in the village. If Banks had entertained thoughts of doing so, he had not dared.

She had asked them to sing the words as a prayer if they could, and each man sang with his eyes on his book, and a strange new look of startled purpose was dawning in some faces.

Then they went out into the starlight silently, but first each man paused and shook hands with Margaret as she stood by the door. They had never done this before. They would not have dared to touch her lily hand unless she gave it them now.

The hand-clasps were awkward, some of them, but each one was a kind of pledge of new fealty to her.

Last of all came Byron, his bold eyes dropped. He did not know whether she would touch his hand or not. He stood hesitating before her. It was something new for him to be embarrassed.

"Will you take my Christ for yours?" she said, looking up and comprehending.

"If I know how," he answered brokenly.

Then out came her eager hand, sealing the promise with a warm grasp of friendliness, and Byron walked out of that door, a new sense of honor dawning in his breast.

She turned back to the room, her face bright with feeling. Stephen stood behind her, and, bending as if he had come for that, kissed her on the forehead, and went quickly into his room, shutting the door behind him.

Then Margaret stood alone with Philip.

14

# *The Arrival of a Newcomer*

*"Had I the grace to win the grace*
*Of maiden living all above,*
*My soul would trample down the base*
*That she might have a man to love.*

*"A grace I had no grace to win*
*Knocks now at my half-opened door;*
*Ah! Lord of glory, come Thou in;*
*Thy grace divine is all, and more!"*
—George Macdonald

"I HAVE been thinking," said Philip, a strange
new light in his eyes, as he turned toward her
from the firelight into which he had been
looking, "of what value are unbeliefs? They do
not change facts. I will throw away mine. I will
take your Christ. If there is no Christ, I shall

lose nothing. If there is, I shall have gained all. Margaret, I take your Jesus to-night to be my Saviour."

He said it solemnly, as one utters a vow for eternity; and the girl stood looking up at him, the radiance in her face reflected in his own.

When he had gone to his room that night, he closed the door and knelt down. A strange gladness was in his heart. He found that he did not shrink from praying, but longed to register his vow, to begin his new life.

"O Christ!" he murmured, reaching out longing arms as if to grope for and find the desire of his heart, "O Christ! Come to me! Show me! Let me know Thou art here. Let me never go back to doubting. I will give Thee all myself, though it is worth but little. Only come to me! Jesus! Jesus! I take Thee as my Saviour!"

It was a different prayer from what he might have prayed if he had not known Margaret. Even if his will and desire had been stirred to praying at all without her influence, he would not have used such language, he would not have spoken to Jesus, the Christ, if he had not heard Margaret's simple, earnest talks of Him every Sunday. He would naturally have spoken to God more distantly, his praying would have been less insistent, and perhaps he would not so soon have received the blessing.

Some one has said that prayer is the throwing of the arms of the soul about the neck of God.

Philip had laid his soul before the Christ, and all tenderly, as if the great arms of God had folded about Him, there came to his soul a sense of the presence of Jesus.

"How sweet the name of Jesus sounds in a believer's ear!" they had sung once in the Sunday class, and Philip had curled his lip quietly, in his corner behind the piano, over the sentiment. How could it be possible that the name of One who has never been seen could be dear, no matter how much one believed?

But now in the new, sweet dawn of his own second birth he suddenly knew that the name "Jesus" was sweet to him. How it had come about, he could not explain. He said it over and over, gently at first, for he feared the sweetness might depart, and then more confidently, as his soul rang with the joy of it. It was true, after all, and one could feel Jesus' presence just as Margaret had said.

With a sense of great peace upon him he lay down at last to rest, but before he closed his eyes in sleep he murmured,

"I thank Thee for sending—Margaret!" and he spoke the name lingeringly and reverently.

They did not say much to each other, Philip and Margaret, about the wonderful change that had come into Philip's heart; but there was a secret understanding between them that made their eyes look glad when they met across the room, and Margaret's heart sang a little song of triumph as she went about her work. It was not for several days that Philip dared to tell her he was beginning to get the answer to his prayer that she had promised, and how he knew that now what she had said was true.

The days went by in much the same way that the preceding ones had gone, save that both Margaret and Philip exercised a more vigorous watchfulness over Stephen. The evenings were spent in delightful readings, and Margaret invented all sorts of little things she wanted made, which the young men could work at while she read.

Margaret was getting to be a good rider since her adventure by night. It seemed to have freed her from all fear, and constantly the three rode about the country together, enjoying the clear, crisp days as the winter hastened on.

It was about this time that there came to

that region a young minister, who had broken down in his first charge, and who had come out to the West to fight nervous prostration on a cattle-ranch. He was an earnest young fellow with no foolish notions, and he had not been long at his new home before he had made friends of the men with whom he was constantly thrown. He had a desire to do them good in some way, though it must be confessed he saw little hope for any such thing. He did not feel well enough to preach, even if there had been any encouragement for starting religious services on Sunday. There seemed to be no church within possible reach, and he pondered much as he rode, and laughed, and learned, of the rough men who gave him no easy lessons, how to rub off the "tenderfoot" looks and ways.

At last, one day he questioned a man from his own ranch. Was there no service of any kind held in the whole of that region? Did they not know of even a Sunday school? Surely there were some Christian people.

The man whom he happened to question was Banks.

Now Banks had been growing exceedingly unpopular among the members of the select Sunday class which met with Margaret Halstead, because he did not take kindly to the extreme principles she taught, nor yield up his rights in the matter of drinking and gambling as some of the others were discussing the possibility of doing. He had made one or two attempts to raise an opposition to the power of the fair young priestess, but they had not been successful. He felt his loss of prestige, and with a half-idea of revenge by getting the minister on his side, and running him in opposition to the young teacher, he began to tell him about the Sunday school.

Banks had a gift of imitation, and a vein of what he supposed was humor. He used them both in this case, and the result was not to the advantage of the Sunday school. However, the young theologue was not altogether without some insight into character. He did not take all that Banks told him as strictly true; and, when the fellow wound up by offering to take him around to the school the next Sunday, he decided to accept the invitation. It would at least give him a chance to study the men and see what influence was able to hold them. It also held out the only opening for a religious service that the neighborhood afforded.

"But you must wear your outfit things, or the boys'll get on to you bein' a preacher, an' make it hot fer ye," said Banks. "They won't have any snobs around. The teacher might think you'd come to break up the meeting, and Earle might take a notion to put you out the back door."

The minister wondered what kind of a strange Sunday school this might be to which he was to be taken; but he quietly accepted the advice, and the next Sunday just as the opening hymn was being sung—Banks had timed his coming well, when all would be occupied and there would be none to dispute the appearance of the newcomer—they walked into the room and sat down.

The minister looked about him in wonder on the beauty and refinement everywhere visible, but his eyes were held at once by the loveliness of the girl who, dressed in soft white, presided over this motley gathering. His eyes went from the hard faces of the men to her pure profile, in wonder, again and again.

There was an ease and mark of the world about the minister, even in his cowboy garb, that Philip noted at once. He drew his brows together in almost his old frown of displeasure as he watched him covertly, jealous of the looks the minister cast at Margaret, jealous of his easy way of smiling and accepting the book that Banks handed him open to the place. It was not till the name "Jesus," repeated several times in a chorus that was being sung, reached Philip's heart, and felt for that vibrating chord that was learning to thrill with joy over the name of his Master, that he realized what an ugly feeling toward this utter stranger had sprung up within him all unbidden. He tried to down it, and looked about for some hospitality to offer the visitor, but in spite of himself he felt dismay at the presence of this man. He was different from the other fellows, and Margaret would see it at once.

Fortunately for Margaret she had no time to look the stranger over closely until after the lesson was done; else she might have been disconcerted. She had long ago overcome her fear of the men she taught every Sabbath, through her intense desire to lead them to the Saviour; but, had she known that her audience that afternoon contained a full-fledged minister fresh from a long theological training, she would have trembled and halted, and perhaps have had no message to deliver that day.

She went through it all as usual, the solemn, silent waiting, and the simple, earnest prayer; and the young minister felt that there were things he had yet to learn about preaching which might not be learned in any theological seminary.

She found him out as soon as he spoke to her, however, which was at the close of the lesson and while they were passing the usual cups of delicious tea and the cakes. She knew him for one of her own world, and welcomed him pleasantly.

Now the minister was small and slight. In contrast with Philip and Stephen and the others he looked insignificant to Margaret's eyes, newly grown accustomed to this giant build of men. So, when he asked permission to come to the class sometimes, she did not feel the trepidation that she would have felt before she came out here. He positively declined to teach. He said his physician had forbidden anything of the sort, and he thanked her warmly for all the help she had given him that afternoon. She found afterwards that he had left her with the impression that he needed help, too. He did not seem to have the same idea about a personal friendship with Jesus Christ that had grown so dear to her.

She felt strengthened, however, at the thought of another Christian to help in the work, and began at once to plan how she would ask him to explain deep points in the lessons that she might in turn explain them to the class. He seemed a bright, interesting young man. Margaret was glad he had come. He was from near her own home, also, and knew many of her intimate friends. That made him doubly interesting.

As the winter went on, the minister began to drop in upon them at sunset, occasionally, to spend the evening. Stephen had taken a fancy to him, and encouraged his coming. Margaret rejoiced at this, and made the minister more welcome because Stephen liked him.

During the long evenings they would read and talk and have music, much as when they were alone.

The minister naturally gravitated to a seat beside Margaret. It was his hand that turned the music for her when she played, and his voice that joined in the duets they sang, for he was something of a musician as well as theologian.

He was also a good reader, and often took the book from Margaret, and read while she rested or busied her hands with a bit of embroidery.

Occasionally the entire Sunday class would be invited for an evening of reading and song. At such times the minister proved to be an admirable helper, always ready with some witty saying or a good recitation. He had the power of whistling in imitation of different birds, and would whistle wild, sweet tunes to a running accompaniment on the piano.

He was not altogether unpopular among the men. He had the sense to keep any extra self-esteem he might have brought out West well locked away in his breast, carrying about with him always a hearty friendliness. The men could not help liking him, and Margaret more and more turned to him for advice and looked for his help in planning for her different gatherings. But when he was present Philip was always silent and gloomy.

Three times during that winter did Stephen grow restless and slip away. Twice his faithful guardians came galloping after him when he was scarcely out of sight of the house, and took him on a long ride that ended only late at night, when they all were worn out; but they brought him safely back, sober. The third time he met Bennett on his way, who immediately suspected and shadowed him till he made sure, whereupon he laid strong hands upon Stephen, and insisted on riding home with him.

Margaret had hoped and prayed. She had even ventured to talk with Stephen at dusk sometimes, when he would come in and throw himself down upon the couch by the fire. He always listened, but he said very little. Not much hope had she ever received from him that he was paying heed to her earnest pleading to come to Jesus Christ and be a new man.

And the winter wore away into the spring.

15

## *Stephen Shows How Strong He Is*

*"All I could never be,*
*All, men ignored in me,*
*This, I was worth to God."*
    —*Robert Browning*

IT was one day in early summer that the minister and Stephen set out on a long ride. They were to return in time for supper, and Margaret had planned a pleasant evening for them all. "The boys," as the Sunday class were now called, were all coming.

She stood watching them ride away into the pleasant afternoon light, and wondered whether the minister would improve his opportunity to say a word to Stephen. She felt very sad about her brother. He did not seem to get any further toward eternal life.

Philip was to have gone with the riding party; but a message in the morning had called him in another direction to attend to some business, and he would not return till evening.

Margaret watched the two riders out of sight, and then went in to finish her plans for the evening. There were one or two little things she wanted to do for an unusual attraction. She was always thinking of new things to win these men into another world than the one they lived in every day.

The two riders went to a distant ranch famed for its superior cattle. They passed spots of marvellous beauty on the way, and stopped to look and wonder; and the minister did improve his opportunity to speak a few earnest words to Stephen, as Margaret had hoped he would do.

Stephen answered sadly, half wistfully, but would not commit himself. He did not repel the words, and seemed to like his companion even better that he had dared to speak.

They spent some time going about the ranch, and late in the afternoon turned their horses homeward.

They had gone about half-way back when a messenger overtook them to beg the minister to return. A whisper had gone around the place that one of the visitors was a minister. The mother of one of the men was lying very ill, not likely to live, and she begged that he would return to pray with her. The message, scrawled feebly, was so pitiful that no one, least of all the kind-hearted young minister, could refuse.

Stephen insisted upon going back with him, but this Mr. Owen would not allow. He said that Stephen must go home and tell his sister the circumstances. He would come as soon as possible. The messenger offered a fresh horse and an escort for returning, and the minister said he would be with them before the evening was over. It would not do for Stephen to go with him, as his sister would wait supper and it would spoil all their plans.

It was a disappointment to the young man, and a deep one. All day as he rode through the brilliant air his heart had been rejoicing over the thought of the evening. He had formed a little plan during the past week, that to-night he would ask Margaret to ride with him some day soon. Then he could have her all to himself, and perhaps—that was as far as he let his thoughts go in the presence of others. He liked to be by himself when he thought of Margaret.

Many miles away there rode another man,

thinking of Margaret, too, and of the minister, sometimes letting his heart rejoice over the smile the girl had given him and the little wave of her white hand in farewell as he rode away that morning, sometimes feeling the heavy gloom of foreboding as a vision of the delicate, spirituelle face of the minister rose before him. For Philip had long known that he loved Margaret better than his own life. Now and then he lifted his eyes up to the clear blue overhead, and called from his heart to his Father, and her Father, not praying, not asking for anything for himself, for he did not dare do that, but just to assure himself that there was a heavenly Father who belonged to them both, who loved them both, and would do well. More than this he did not venture to think.

Stephen sat in his saddle, watching his friend out of sight on the road they had just come together. He felt a strong impulse even yet to turn and follow him. Something told him it would be better. Something whispered that here was his safety. He half called to them as they disappeared around a knoll; and then, remembering that Margaret would be watching anxiously for them, and determining for once to show he was a man and could be trusted, he reluctantly started his horse on alone.

But the devil came also.

The devil had not had so good a chance at Stephen for nearly a year. He had been watching his opportunity, and had almost given up this soul that was once so firmly in his clutches. But now he came swiftly, and attended him with all his old arts and many more beside. He whispered:

"You'd better ride around by the town, and go through, and then you can tell Margaret how strong you are."

That was the first thought. Ride through town, and not go into the saloon, nor stop once to talk to any one! He would enjoy knowing that he could do that. He might even try to be the Christian Margaret and the minister wanted him to be if he could do that once. He would not be so ashamed. He half decided he would do it, and turned it over in his mind, that mind so easily influenced by his own imagination that to think of going through town was almost as much of a temptation as going. He could see how the saloon-keeper would stand at the door and look, and wonder, and perhaps call. He could smell the odor of the familiar room as it was wafted out into the road from the swinging blind door.

Something wild seized him with the

thought of that odor. A spirit that would not be downed. He forgot that he had intended to ride safely through town to astonish and please his sister by his strength. He forgot his half-desire to be a Christian. He forgot the words the minister had spoken, which indeed had taken deep hold upon his wavering nature. He forgot everything save that one fiendish thirst for strong drink, and he set the spurs cruelly into his faithful horse, and rode like mad, his breath coming in great, hot waves through his lungs. His eyes grew blood-shot, and all the devils in the service of the arch-fiend flew to urge him on. There were miles yet to be covered, but that was nothing. He was alone and unsuspected. He had time to get there and get all he wanted. All he wanted! For once no one could stop him, for no one would know until the minister came back, and that might not be to-night.

He turned upon a road that would not lead past home, and galloped on. It was the road his sister had taken in her wild night ride after him and Philip.

It was quite dusk when he neared the bridge that she had crossed in safety and but just escaped with her life. He knew the bridge had long been disused. He knew that it was considered extremely unsafe. He did not know of the great supporting timber that had parted and fallen into the ravine below on the night Margaret had crossed. But he knew enough about it to make him feel even in his most daring moods, heretofore, that he would rather not try to cross it.

But something stronger than reason was urging him to-night. This bridge would lead to a crossroad where he would not be in danger of meeting any of the fellows coming up to Margaret's gathering. The fellows had of late been a sort of self-constituted watch-guard. He could not shake them off. They had kept him many a time from himself. He would escape them all to-night. The fever in his blood had taken fire through all his veins. A blind purpose took possession of his reason.

With sudden quick jerk of the bridle he turned his trembling horse, and put him at the bridge, nor would he let him lessen his gait. He half knew in his wild folly that his safety lay in getting over quickly, if safety there was. And so under full gallop the panting horse flew at the bridge in the fast-gathering darkness.

It wavered and cracked, and wavered long, and then suddenly, too late, the horse drew back upon his haunches with a frightened snort almost human in its anguish, and poised a moment in mid-air! The bridge did not reach across the chasm! One whole section had fallen! The last support was tottering in decay!

One awful second Stephen realized his position, and saw in vivid panorama the follies of his life and the sins of his heart. Saw, and cried out in one wild cry to God, in acknowledgment and late submission. The cry rang through the upper air, down into the dark ravine; then all was blackness of unconsciousness to Stephen as bridge, horse, and rider fell crashing below!

The supper had stood waiting for some time when Philip came. Margaret was growing restless, and was glad to see him. His face was anxious when he heard that the riders had not returned, though he tried to laugh it off and say the minister was not used to long rides. Perhaps it had been too much for him, and they had had to stop to rest; but in another half hour Mr. Owen, his horse all covered with froth, rode gayly up to the door, and dismounted.

He made his apologies, explained his lateness, and then looked around for Stephen.

"Isn't he here yet?" he asked in surprise.

But there was more than surprise in the faces of the other two. There was trouble. Philip excused himself immediately, and went toward the barn. His own horse was weary with the long, hard day. He must take the other horse. He saddled it, and quickly led it out into the darkness; but at the door stood Margaret, her face white and drawn, a steady purpose in her eyes. Philip could see it shining through the starlight like another star. She had followed him to the barn, intending to ride with him after Stephen.

He dropped the horse's bridle, and came over to her. Taking both her cold little hands in his strong ones, he looked down into her face.

"Margaret," he said, and there was deep tenderness in his tone, "I know what you would do, but you must not. You must promise me you will stay here and pray. You cannot go out into the night this way. There is no need, and I will not let you. I will not go myself until you promise."

She caught her breath in a half-sob, and dropped her face miserably upon his hands that held hers so firmly.

He drew her to him in the shadow of the great, dark barn, and, bending over her, kissed reverently the silken coils of hair upon her head. "Margaret, I love you; will you do this for me? Will you promise to stay at home and pray?"

He was half frightened afterward that he had dared to speak to her so, but she did not shrink away. Instead, she stood very still, and held her breath for a moment, and then answered low and sweet,

"Yes, Philip!"

He longed to take her in his arms, but he dared not. He gave her hands one long, tender clasp, and sprang into his saddle; but Margaret's white face looked up now, and she ran a step or two beside the horse. She clasped her hands in pleading.

"You will be careful, Philip—for yourself," she said brokenly, and his heart leaped with joy as he promised. Yet, after all, he told himself it might be only a sisterly care.

She watched him ride away through the dark, her hand at her throat to still the wild, sweet, fluttering thing of joy that had come to thrill her soul. And for the minute she half forgot her fears for Stephen in love and fear for Philip. She stood still several minutes, and let the memory of his kiss flow over her and cover her with its glory and its joy. Then she went swiftly in, and tried to entertain the minister, who was wondering and rejoicing that he had her to himself for a little while. Poor soul, he did not know her thoughts were far out down the dark road, following a rider through the night.

As Philip rode along, he could not believe that he had really dared to tell Margaret that he loved her. It seemed too strange and wonderful to be true that she had not repulsed him when he kissed her. As the tumult in his heart quieted a little to let him think, he told himself that perhaps she was excited about Stephen, and had needed comfort. She had not realized what his words of love had meant. It might be she only took his meaning as a kind and brotherly feeling. If that were so, he would never take an advantage of her. That moment they had spent together should be a sacred thing between them. He would rejoice always in that kiss and that chance to hold her dear white hands.

But wild and sweet through such thoughts thrilled the joy of loving her and the song of hope in his heart. For something every now and then made him sure that she loved him, marvellous as it might seem.

So he rode down through the dark into

town, and, finding no trace of Stephen nor any one who had seen him, turned his horse back to the house to see whether he had come; anxious now and grave, canvassing every possible way to turn next for the finding of Stephen. Then he remembered, and began to pray for guidance and help.

Stephen's wild cry had reached the ears of two men travelling along the upper road above the ravine with a wagon. They stopped, listened, and heard the crashing timbers and fall of horse and man.

Instinct taught them what the accident must be, and they went to find out who it was that had fallen to a death so sudden. They carried a lantern; for the night was dark, and one was old, and the road they had to go was treacherous in some places. So now, when they could see only the blackness of horror below, they climbed down another way, leaving their horse tied above, and found the place where Stephen lay.

The horse was dead, and lay quite motionless with all his four faithful legs broken and a great beam of rotten timber across one temple, where it struck and mercifully ended his life.

But Stephen lay a little further off, flung, partly by the struggles of his horse, perhaps, or it may have been by some wild leap of his own in the moment of falling. He was stretched upon a grassy place, the kindest that the old ravine could offer, and lay unscratched apparently, the damp gold waves of hair lying loose upon his forehead, his hands flung out as if he were asleep. He was profoundly unconscious of the majesty in which he lay.

The men held the lantern to his face, and one muttered with a great oath:

"Steve Halstead! Drunk again!"

They tore his shirt open, and felt for his heart, but could not tell whether he was dead or living. Finally they carried him with great difficulty up a sloping, circuitous path, and put him in the wagon.

Bennett and Byron and two or three others had just arrived when they brought him in. Margaret turned away in sick horror. She had never seen her brother drunk. She could not bear to look now. They motioned her from the door, and laid him upon his own bed; but something in his face made Byron stoop down. There was no breath of liquor upon him. They listened with shocked faces as the two who had found him told their story. Then Byron flung himself upon his horse, and galloped off into the night for the doctor, while the others worked in desperation to bring him to consciousness, with the door closed against his sister.

It was Bennett who told Margaret that her brother had had a fall on the way home, and that he had not been to the village at all, but was found on his way there. Her face lighted at that. She understood his meaning. She was glad Stephen had not been drinking. They sent the minister to stay with her; and she was wide-eyed and brave, and would talk but little, looking anxiously through the open front door.

There came a sound of horses presently, and she rushed out into the night. Mr. Owen thought she was looking for the doctor, and let her go, thinking it might be well for her to have something to do, even if it were nothing but to watch for the doctor, who could not possibly have come so soon.

It was Philip who had come.

She ran out to him, and looked anxiously through the dark.

"O Philip, is it you? And are you safe?"

And Philip's heart warmed with hope.

"They have brought him home, Philip. He had fallen through the bridge. I was afraid you had fallen, too. I do not know how badly he is hurt; but, Philip, he had not been drinking!"

There was a ring of triumph in her last words, as if it could not be all bad, whatever might be coming. Then together they went into the house.

"She is a wonderful girl, isn't she?" said the minister to Philip in subdued tones a little later, as he watched her go quietly about getting a cup of tea for Philip. "It seems so strange that I should have had to come away out here to find her, when our native towns were but twenty miles apart." In his voice was a tone of possession and pride, and Philip's heart sank as he listened.

16

## *Stephen's Life Goes On*

THE DOCTOR came by and by, and was able to bring back the spirit into the form that had lain so still and deathlike. Stephen opened his eyes, and looked about him with a bewildered gaze as of one who had expected a different scene. He looked first at his sister, who had come into the room with the doctor, and then he smiled.

"I didn't get there, though, Margaret," he murmured. "God stopped me on the way. It was the only way He could save me."

He closed his eyes, and they thought he had fainted again; but he opened them with his old, careless, mischievous smile, and looked around upon the boys, his eyes lingering lovingly on Philip's face.

"I've been a coward, boys," he said, "and I've

tried to get away from Him all the time; but still He kept drawing me, and you all helped. And now He's going to take me to Himself. There won't be any more drinks up there, and maybe I can begin over again."

The words were faint, and the doctor bent over him and administered a stimulant.

He made a thorough examination, and told them that Stephen was hurt internally and could not live long. They thought he was not conscious; but he opened his eyes, and smiled at them.

"It's all right, doctor. It's better so," he said feebly. "But can't you give me something to strengthen me up for a few hours? I've got something I want to say to the boys."

The doctor turned away to rub his hand across his eyes; and the men moved, choking, away from the bed, and went to the windows or slipped into the other room.

"I'll try!" said the doctor huskily. "If you'll lie quiet and rest a little, you may live through the night."

Stephen obediently took the medicine, and lay quiet for a few minutes; but as soon as the artificial strength came to him he began to talk. The gay, reckless tongue that had been the life of so many gatherings had but a little while longer to speak.

It was Philip who came to him first, and tried to quiet him with that strong personality that had so often saved him from himself.

But Stephen's mind was abnormally active. He seemed to think of things he had neglected all his life. He spoke of this and that he would like to have Philip do for him, and he talked tenderly of his sister.

"You'll look after her, Philip?" he asked anxiously. "You know she'll have no one now when I'm gone. She will be sorry. You like her, don't you?"

Philip's eyes filled with tears, and his strong chin quivered.

"I love her, Stephen, with all my soul," he said with choking voice. "I will care for her as far as she will let me care. I will make her my wife if she will consent."

"Consent?" said Stephen, his voice rising and his old petulant manner coming back to him, as ever when his will was crossed in the slightest. "Consent! Of course she will! Why shouldn't she? No one could help admiring you, Phil. Why can't you be married right away, before I go? I'd like to see it. I'd like to give you my blessing."

He looked up eagerly into Philip's face.

Philip almost groaned.

"Why can't you, Phil?" he urged again.

"I have not asked her yet," said Philip. "She may not love me at all. Sometimes I think she loves the minister."

"Then ask her now," said Stephen, and he called in the high, thin voice of those who are almost done with life, "Margaret!"

She heard his cry through the slight partitions, and came at once.

Stephen had almost exhausted his breath with his eagerness, and lay panting, looking up first at Philip wistfully, then at his sister.

"Phil—has something—to tell you," he gasped, and then swallowed the spoonful Philip gave him from the glass the doctor had left, and closed his eyes.

Philip scarcely dared to look at Margaret. It seemed almost a desecration in this hour of death to speak of what meant life and joy to him.

"I have been telling Stephen of my love for you," he said, trying to control the tremble in his voice. "I have been saying I would like to make you my wife. I would not dare intrude this upon you now, but Stephen longs to know how you feel about it."

Philip had come near her, and they both stood close to Stephen's side. There was an undertone of pity for her in Philip's voice as he spoke, and a slight touch of formality in his words because of the presence of a third person, that made it seem like a contract in writing. But Margaret remembered his impassioned tones a little while before in the shadow of the night, and did not doubt his deep love for her.

With the tears brimming her eyes she looked up to Philip, and tried to smile. Her lips were trembling with emotion, but she said simply,

"I love you, Philip!" and put her hands out to his.

Then Stephen's great brown hand, so weak now, came groping out to them and clasped them both, and the two with one consent knelt down beside his bed.

"Be married now, while I am here," he whispered. "I can leave you better so." He looked pleadingly at them.

Margaret caught her breath with a sob, and Philip put his arm tenderly about her.

"Can you bear to—dear?" he asked.

She was still a minute with drooping face and downcast eyes, and then she whispered softly,

"Yes."

Philip stooped and kissed her forehead reverently, and Stephen smiled his old joyous smile. For a minute the shadow of death that was beginning to hover over his face was chased away.

"Where are the boys?" he asked. "I want the boys and the minister. I'll tell them. No, it won't be too hard. I'd like to. Go and get ready."

They came trooping in, the great, rough men who loved him, and who had tried so hard to ruin him and save him both. The minister came behind them, and the doctor hurried in and felt Stephen's pulse. But he did not notice the doctor. He was all eagerness.

"Boys, we're going to have a wedding!" he said in a cheery, weak voice. They thought his mind was wandering, and looked sorrowfully at one another.

"That's all right, boys," he said as he saw they did not understand. "It's sure enough. I want you to carry me into the other room for the ceremony. No, don't say they can't, Doc. I'll stay alive long enough to say all I need to say. I must go out there where we've had so many good times. I'd rather die out there. Take me out, boys; we've no time to waste. Philip and

Margaret are out there waiting, and the minister will marry them."

His old impatience was using up his strength fast. The doctor looked grave, but said in a low tone:

"Take him out. It cannot make much difference."

They gathered up the mattress tenderly, the clumsy fellows, and carried it out to a cot that was placed across in front of the fireplace. Almost they thought he was gone when they laid him down; but he rallied wonderfully, and, smiling, whispered,

"Go on."

Philip and Margaret, quiet and white, stood together, hand in hand, in front of the mass of summer blossoms that Margaret had arranged a few hours before for the expected evening gathering. It was just where she had sat to teach their first Sunday class, and she was all in white as then. There was a glorified light in her eyes that defied the sadness even of death. Stephen wondered as he looked at her whether she was looking up to and speaking with the unseen presence of her Christ.

The room was beautiful, and only Stephen as he lay with partly closed eyes and watched them, half impatient for the ceremony to be

over, remembered the bare old room filled
with the odor of lamp-smoke and bacon into
which they had brought his sister on the night
of her arrival. And in his heart he thanked God
for her coming.

The minister with stricken look and
trembling voice performed the ceremony. It
was hard for life to take away his love just as
death was stealing a good friend. He had
begun his portion of sorrow, and would learn
his lesson; but it was bitter at the start.

There in the "chill before the dawning,
between the night and morning," while the
angel of Death delayed a little, to watch, they
were married. The night was black around the
little house, and the stars kept watch above.

As soon as it was over, and the short prayer
ended, Stephen made a movement as if to rise,
and then, remembering, dropped his head
again.

"Boys, I can't stay long," he said eagerly. "I
only stayed for the wedding," and he smiled in
his old, reckless way. Then, growing sober, with
an honest ring to his voice that sometimes
came in his speech so winningly, he said:

"There's something I want you to do, boys.
You can if you only will. I want you to promise
me before I go. I want you to build a church

here, and get the minister to run it. You can do it well enough if you don't go to the saloon. It's the saloon, boys, and the gambling, that has taken all our money, and made us into such beasts. It was the saloon that ruined me. You all know that. You all know how I came here and bought this place, and then drank it all up and everything else I had, and would have gone to the devil at once if it hadn't been for Phil coming out and buying back the place, and keeping me half-way straight."

His breath was growing short. His sentences became more broken.

"You all know what my sister's done for me," he went on. "God bless her. But even she couldn't save me. The devil had too tight a hold. I'm sorry I didn't do as she wanted me to, and take Jesus Christ—it might have done some good—but now it's too late—He'll just have to take me. I guess He'll do it. I've made a clean breast of it—but it's been a wasted life. Don't wait any longer, boys. I've thought if there'd been a church here when I came—and a minister—who lived right up to what he said—it might not have been so with me. Now, boys, will you build the church?"

They had turned away to hide the tears that were coursing down their bronzed faces; but they went solemnly, one at a time, and took his cold hand in a strong grasp, and made the promise in hoarse, broken murmurs.

"That's all right, then, boys. I know you'll do it," said Stephen; "and, boys," with almost a twinkle of the old mischief in his eyes, "I want them to put me on the hill here under the big tree, and mark the place so you'll remember your promise. I'll maybe be able to help a little that way by reminding, and so make up for all I've wasted."

He was still a minute. His voice kept its strength wonderfully.

"Sing, boys," he said, opening his eyes. "Sing all the old songs. It will make me feel more at home where I'm going to hear your voices on the way."

They looked helplessly at one another. They did not know what to sing.

"Sing 'Jesus, Saviour, pilot me,' boys," he said. "I didn't live for Him, but maybe I can die with Him."

Tremblingly the great voices started, like some grand organ that has lost its player, and creaks on feebly at the touch of sorrow with a broken heart.

When they were through, he said:

"Sing 'Safe home in port.' I always liked that.

And, boys, sing it as if you were glad. Sing it as you always do."

Then they mastered themselves and sang:

> *"Safe home, safe home, in port!*
> *Rent cordage, shattered deck,*
> *Torn sails, provisions short,*
> *And only not a wreck;*
> *But, O, the joy, upon the shore,*
> *To tell the voyage perils o'er!"*

They were singing as they used to sing it in those first bright Sundays, now. Something of the spirit of the triumph in the song had caught them.

> *"No more the foe can harm!*
> *No more the leaguered camp,*
> *And cry of night alarm,*
> *And need of ready lamp;*
> *And yet how nearly had he failed,*
> *How nearly had the foe prevailed!"*

"That's right, boys! That's me! It's all true," called out Stephen to them. They could see the shadow deepening about his eyes now.

Their voices grew softer with tenderness, but they sang on. They would sing him right grandly into heaven if that was what he wanted, even if it broke their hearts. Their voices should not fail him while he could listen.

>*"The exile is at home!*
>*Oh, nights and days of tears!"*

Stephen pressed Margaret's hand that lay in his, at these words, and she tenderly kissed him.

>*"Oh, longings not to roam!*
>*Oh, sins and doubts and fears!*
>*What matters now grief's darkest day*
>*When God has wiped all tears away?"*

It was the minister who started other hymns, words that he had heard them sing in their gatherings. They needed no books, nor could they have looked at them with their tear-blinded eyes, if they had them.

Stephen was sinking fast. He did not talk any more, nor look at them. Once he opened his eyes, and, looking at Margaret, murmured, "Dear sister!"

He had lain so still for a long time that they thought he had ceased breathing, when he suddenly opened his eyes, and with a strength born of his flight into another world raised himself from the pillow, calling in a loud, clear voice:

"Did you call, father? Yes, sir, I'm coming!"

Then he fell back dead.

Was it some memory of his boyhood that came to him at last, or did he hear his heavenly Father's voice?

It was the minister that started to sing,

*"Safe in the arms of Jesus,*
*Safe on His gentle breast";*

and with choking sobs that did not need to be suppressed the men joined in the song that Stephen loved. Just then the sun shot up behind the hills, and laid a touch of glory on the gold of Stephen's hair.

"He is safe home in Port," said the minister. "Let us pray."

They knelt about him in their grief, and heard him pray for them, and then went out and left Philip and Margaret with their sorrow and their joy.

They went out to a new world wherein were vows to be kept and a goal to be attained, and each man was resolved to do his best to keep the sacred trust that Stephen had left to them.

They went about among Stephen's friends, and gathered up a goodly sum. They brought it to Margaret on the day of the funeral service, and told her it was for the church, and that it should be built at once. Margaret, smiling through her tears, thanked God, and knew her prayers were being answered.

They laid him in the place he had spoken of under the great tree that crowned the hill, and to mark it they put a stone whereon were engraved Stephen's name, the date, and the simple words, "Safe Home."

Beside the grave up rose the little church, its spire pointing heavenward, its doors stretched wide to save both day and night, its bell calling over the lonely country at set times of worship, and over the door, cut into the stone, the words,

"Stephen Halstead Memorial."

The minister has found his church; and Stephen's life, though gathered safe home, is going on in the memory of those he is helping.

THE END.

## About the Author

Grace Livingston Hill is well known as one of the most prolific writers of romantic fiction. Her personal life was fraught with joys and sorrows not unlike those experienced by many of her fictional heroines.

Born in Wellsville, New York, Grace nearly died during the first hours of life. But her loving parents and friends turned to God in prayer. She survived miraculously; thus her thankful father named her Grace.

Grace was always close to her father, a Presbyterian minister, and her mother, a published writer. It was from them that she learned the art of storytelling. When Grace was twelve, a close aunt surprised her with a hardbound, illustrated copy of one of Grace's stories. This was the beginning of Grace's journey into being a published author.

In 1892 Grace married Fred Hill, a young minister, and they soon had two lovely young daughters. Then came 1901, a difficult year for Grace—the year when, within months of each other, both her father and her husband died. Suddenly Grace had to find a new place to live (her home was owned by the church where her husband had been pastor). It was a struggle for Grace to raise her young daughters alone, but through everything she kept writing. In 1902 she produced *The Angel of His Presence, The Story of a Whim,* and *An Unwilling Guest.* In 1903 her two books *According to the Pattern* and *Because of Stephen* were published.

It wasn't long before Grace was a well-known author, but she wanted to go beyond just entertaining her readers. She soon included the message of God's salvation through Jesus Christ in each of her books. For Grace, the most important thing she did was not write books but share the message of salvation, a message she felt God wanted her to share through the abilities he had given her.

In all, Grace Livingston Hill wrote more than one hundred books, all of which have sold thousands of copies and have touched the lives of readers around the world with their message of "enduring love" and the true way to lasting happiness: a relationship with God through his Son, Jesus Christ.

In an interview shortly before her death, Grace's devotion to her Lord still shone clear. She commented that whatever she had accomplished had been God's doing. She was only his servant, one who had tried to follow his teaching in all her thoughts and writing.

# Don't miss these Grace Livingston Hill romance novels!

You can find Tyndale books at fine bookstores everywhere. If you are unable to find these titles at your local bookstore, you may write for ordering information to:

**Tyndale House Publishers**
**Tyndale Family Products Dept.**
**Box 448**
**Wheaton, IL 60189**